Praise for

ZOMBIE BASEBALL BEATDOWN

A 2014 LOCUS AWARD FINALIST

"A rip-roaring romp of real-life sports and undead zombies that **gives us so much more to chew over than human flesh**."
—Gordon Korman, author of *Schooled* and *Swindle*

"**Simultaneously smart, funny, and icky**, this book asks a tough question: Is it worth looking the other way in order to save yourself?" —*Booklist*

"Upton Sinclair's *The Jungle* meets *Left 4 Dead*/*The Walking Dead*/ *Shaun of the Dead* in **a high-energy, high-humor look at the zombie apocalypse**." —*Kirkus Reviews*

"Printz-winner Bacigalupi...defies the expectations of the comedy-horror genre, turning this zombie novel into **an effective bit of social commentary** while staying true to the story's grisly and goofy roots.... Casual **readers will have a blast**, and those who look deeper will learn something, too." —*Publishers Weekly*

"**Thought-provoking**, topical issues and **wry wit** elevate [this] above the expected gross-out zombie tale....Rabi, Miguel, and Joe are realistic, complete characters. It's a testament to the author's skill that they express **values of courage, friendship, and integrity** as naturally as they toss off hilarious observations....[A] **fast-paced home run**." —*School Library Journal*

"This zombie tale is satisfyingly **funny in all of the middle-school boy ways** and gory enough to please fans of *Left 4 Dead*....**A dark comedy with a bit of heart**." —*The Bulletin*

"**Kids will devour this** like a zombie would a plate of fresh brains."
—*Shelf Awareness*

ZOMBIE BASEBALL BEATDOWN

PAOLO BACIGALUPI

LITTLE, BROWN AND COMPANY

New York · Boston

This book is a work of fiction. Names, characters, places, and incidents are the product
of the author's imagination or are used fictitiously. Any resemblance to actual events, locales,
or persons, living or dead, is coincidental.

Copyright © 2013 by Paolo Bacigalupi
Discussion Guide copyright © 2014 by Little, Brown and Company
Author Interview copyright © 2014 by Paolo Bacigalupi
"How to Survive the (Next) Zombie Apocalypse" copyright © 2013 by
Little, Brown and Company

All rights reserved. In accordance with the U.S. Copyright Act of 1976, the scanning,
uploading, and electronic sharing of any part of this book without the permission of the
publisher is unlawful piracy and theft of the author's intellectual property. If you would like
to use material from the book (other than for review purposes), prior written permission
must be obtained by contacting the publisher at permissions@hbgusa.com. Thank you for
your support of the author's rights.

Little, Brown and Company

Hachette Book Group
1290 Avenue of the Americas, New York, NY 10104
Visit our website at lb-kids.com

Little, Brown and Company is a division of Hachette Book Group, Inc.
The Little, Brown name and logo are trademarks of Hachette Book Group, Inc.

The publisher is not responsible for websites (or their content) that
are not owned by the publisher.

First Paperback Edition: September 2014
First published in hardcover in September 2013 by Little, Brown and Company

Library of Congress Cataloging-in-Publication Data

Bacigalupi, Paolo.
    Zombie baseball beatdown / by Paolo Bacigalupi.—First edition.
      pages cm
    Summary: While practicing for their next baseball game, thirteen-year-old
friends Rabi, Miguel, and Joe discover that the nefarious activities of the Delbe, Iowa,
meatpacking plant have caused cows to turn into zombies.
    ISBN 978-0-316-22078-1 (hc)—ISBN 978-0-316-22079-8 (pb)
    [1. Zombies—Fiction.   2. Packing-houses—Fiction.   3. East Indian Americans—
Fiction.   4. Racially mixed people—Fiction.]   I. Title.
    PZ7.B132185Zo 2013
    [Fic]—dc23
                                                                                    2012041463

10 9 8 7 6 5 4 3

RRD-C

Printed in the United States of America

For Jobim, who said he wanted to read about zombies;
for Arjun, because it always is;
and for anyone who has ever wanted to save the world

CHAPTER 1

Losing sucks.

Don't let anyone tell you it builds character or any of that junk; it sucks. It sucks that someone else is beating you. It sucks that you've worked so hard and it's going to mean nothing. It sucks that you can't hit the ball the way you want and can't field the grounder the way you imagined—a thousand things about losing suck.

But it sucks worse when you're stuck in the dugout on a 102-degree day in the humidity, and the heat index is 120, and sweat is pouring off you, and your team is losing—not because you suck at baseball, but because your baseball coach, Mr. Cocoran, sucks at coaching.

Mr. Cocoran won't listen to you when you tell him he's got the batting order wrong. He likes big hits and loves guys who hack at the ball and swing for the fences and all that junk, and he doesn't understand about getting runners on base. He doesn't know squat about baseball.

But you know the thing about losing that sucks even worse than that?

Knowing you're the one who's going to get blamed.

When you're finally up at bat, with Miguel on third and Sammy on first, and you're down by two in the bottom of the sixth, and you're the last and final hope of the Delbe Diamondbacks—you're the one everyone is going to remember.

Maybe I could hit a single on my good days (and if the pitcher was off his game), but basically, for me, the ball just moves too darn fast.

My dad says I swing with my heart.

Well, he said that after I struck out once and spun myself all the way around and all the other kids were so busy laughing at me—even my own team—that nobody minded so much that we'd lost another game.

After that game, my dad came up to me and put his hand on my shoulder and said, "Don't worry about it, Rabi; you swung with your heart. You were all in. We can work on your swing. As soon as I'm back from the rigs, we'll work on it."

Of course, baseball season was going to be over by

then, so my swing wasn't going to improve in time to save me from more humiliation. Dad works oil and gas rigs—ten weeks on, two weeks off—so I was on my own.

There was no way I should have been batting cleanup, I can tell you that, but there I was, sitting on the bench, watching the lineup come down to me, like a slow-moving train wreck.

Miguel was sitting next to me, chewing gum. "What're the odds?" he asked.

I shrugged. "I don't know."

"Come on, Rabi." Joe, who was sitting on my other side, poked me in the ribs. "Do that trick you do. With the numbers."

A couple of the older guys, Travis Thompson and Sammy Riggoni, both looked over. Beefy dudes with mean piggy eyes who liked to hassle anyone who was littler than them. I didn't want their attention at all. I looked away.

"Nah," I said. "There's not enough numbers to do it. I need more stats. You can't do stats with Little League. You need a lot of numbers before you can predict anything."

"Come on," Miguel said. "You know you can."

I looked out at the bases, frowning. I studied the batters in our lineup, eyed the Eamons Eagles defense, their catcher and fielders and pitcher. And then I started setting stats. It was a trick I used. I could set stats over the different players' heads in my mind, a little like health bars in *World of Warcraft*, and then I could figure out probable outcomes.

Numbers. Stats. I have a cousin in Boston who calls it my inner Asian math nerd.

But whatever it is, I'm good at it. The Eagles pitcher was still going strong, even after pitching most of the game. We hadn't worn him down much. I'd read up on his stats and seen how he normally did after pitching four innings. I'd been counting how many times he'd actually had to pitch against all our batters, and I knew he wasn't tired. Not a bit.

He'd just struck out Billy Freudenberg on three straight pitches. And now Shawn Carney, at the plate, had two balls and two strikes on him. But Shawn barely hit .225, even against a weak pitcher. Against the Eamons guy, he was more like .075. Shawn was always hacking at random pitches. When he hit, he hit with power, but the Eamons pitcher was smart enough to bait him into swinging at a mean little curveball.

Shawn was dead meat.

Then there'd be Miguel. Miguel was hitting .525 on

the season, steady all the time, dangerous. And the Eamons pitcher was afraid of him. Miguel could get himself on base, for sure. He was a slugger and he hit for extra bases more often than not. After that, Sammy would be up—.305, but not with as much power as Miguel. Then there'd be me. It all added up to...

"You need a double or better," I said. "And Sammy needs the same for us to tie."

Miguel cracked his gum. "And if we do, that means you got to..."

"I got to do anything except strike out. Anything at all."

"What are the odds?"

I laughed. "If you two nail it? Twenty to one, against. If you don't?" I shrugged. "No shot."

"Don't sell yourself short," Miguel said. "You can get on, no problem."

"Numbers don't lie. It wouldn't be a problem if they moved me ahead of you two. I do better when there's no one on base, and no pressure. If Mr. Cocoran would just concentrate on getting players on base, concentrate on getting more walks instead of big hits, we'd already be winning right now. And this wouldn't matter at all. We'd probably be up two at this point. Game over, Delbe wins."

Miguel nodded out at Shawn, who was getting ready for his next pitch. "What if Shawn gets a hit?"

I looked over at the redheaded boy. "He won't. Not with two strikes on him. He always chokes once he gets two strikes."

"Shut up, Rabi. You're on a team."

That was Mr. Cocoran, our king of a coach. Funny-looking guy with a big nose and a face that was red like a tandoori chicken. He was always irritated. Mostly at me. "You don't rip your own teammates," Mr. Cocoran said. "Especially with *your* batting average."

Sammy Riggoni snickered. "Yeah, Rabi, have you even hit a ball this season?"

I think somewhere in the Little League rule book, there's something about being a good sport, and everyone playing hard, and winning clean, and working together as a team. I'm pretty sure it's there, somewhere.

For Mr. Cocoran, that meant telling the good players they were amazing, and pretending the crummy players didn't exist. I mean, sure, I'm a terrible hitter. But so is Shawn. I'm not being mean; the kid's got a serious hole in his swing. When the count's 2–2, he always chokes. It doesn't do any good to stand around clapping and cheering and saying he can do it, after you've spent the entire season ignoring the problem.

6

My dad says there's no point pretending reality doesn't exist; otherwise, you can't fix anything. Mr. Cocoran should have paid attention to Shawn and helped him get better. Instead, he spent his time helping Sammy, because Sammy was a "natural."

That was how Cocoran rolled, and now, under Cocoran's glare, I shut up. I didn't want to argue with him, and I sure didn't want to get in a fight with Sammy. Besides, two seconds later, the numbers lined up, just like I expected, and made my point for me. Shawn hacked at a crummy pitch and popped the ball straight up, and the catcher snagged it nice and easy. Two outs.

Cocoran glared at me even harder.

It's got to be annoying when a middle school kid knows more about baseball than you.

Miguel was up. He went out into the sun, and just like the numbers predicted, he got a hit. He roped a double, which wasn't as good as we needed. Then Sammy singled, which moved Miguel to third. If Sammy had tripled, then we would've had a chance...but no.

It was down to me, walking out to home plate.

It should have been Miguel standing where I was now. The guy who hits a double on his bad day. If Cocoran had changed the batting order, Miguel could have driven runs in all day long. Instead he liked to get Miguel out there early, and tried to get him to steal bases.

Cocoran was standing at the entrance to the dugout, sweating and shouting for me to make it happen. I stood over the plate. The pitcher was looking at me, smirking. He had runners on first and third, which might have worried him, except he was facing me, a batter he'd struck out every time. He knew that I was the end of the inning—and the game.

Miguel was nodding encouragingly, willing me to bring him home. Sammy was just staring at me. I could tell he hated that he had to depend on a shrimp like me to do something right for once. Too bad for him that I'm a strategizer, not a slugger. I *think*. I don't *do*.

The sun pounded down. The stands got quiet.

And then my mom started clapping.

Everyone swung around to look at her.

There she was, up in the stands, calling, "*Rabindra-nath! Ra-bin-dra-nath! Ra-bin-dra-nath!*" This crazy Indian lady in a bright yellow sari, with night-black hair in a bun and a red bindi in the middle of her brown forehead, was cheering for me. She didn't care that everyone was looking at her, or that she was embarrassing me. She was all in, supporting her son.

I wanted to die.

I looked down at the plate, then up at the pitcher. He was grinning at me. He knew he had me now. And that made me mad, him thinking he could just whup me that way.

So what if I had a name no one could pronounce? So what if I had a mom who wore saris? I was going to take his pitch and knock the cover off the ball. I was going to teach them all not to laugh at me.

I looked at the pitcher, and I pointed, just pointed toward left field, letting him know where I was going to put the ball, staring him down, letting him know that I owned him.

Rabindranath Chatterjee-Jones was going to knock the ball out of the park.

Around me, everyone went quiet. Even my mom.

I was ready. I touched the plate. Wound up the bat.

The pitch came in high.

I let it go.

"*Strike one!*" the umpire shouted.

I stepped off the plate, trying not to let it rattle me.

The catcher snickered. "Shoulda swung at that one, huh?"

It didn't matter. I wasn't going to let him get to me. I just needed to think about the bat knocking the stuffing out of the ball.

"You should swing at this next one," the catcher said. "We're trying to make it easy for you, man."

I let the second pitch come by, too, knowing that the Eamons pitcher would try to fool me. It was coming low, this time.

"Strike two!"

What the . . . ? I thought it was a ball, for sure.

But now, here it was: the pitch I'd been waiting for—fast and straight and right down the pipe. Perfect.

I swung like there wasn't ever going to be another tomorrow—and once again, I swung so hard I spun around and tripped over my own tangled legs.

I fell down in a pile.

Everyone groaned.

And that was it. End of the game. Everyone laughing at me . . . Miguel walking toward me, shaking his head . . . my mom, up there in the stands, sitting there like a bright yellow dandelion, looking sad, like I'd disappointed her—even though she never really liked baseball anyway and only cared about cricket . . . and Sammy Riggoni, coming over to me as I started to get up.

To my surprise, Sammy reached down to give me a hand up. I let him pull me upright, but then he jerked me close.

"Coach is right, red dot, you're a crummy hitter," he

10

said in my ear, and then gave me a shove that made me stumble back.

Miguel and Joe saw it happen and charged in to back me up, but then Sammy's friends were there, too. Rob Ziegler and Bill Tuffin and the rest of them, glaring. All of them bigger and stronger than us, except maybe Miguel. There was no way we could beat them. If you stacked up the stats, a fight with Sammy's friends added up to GAME OVER.

"Come on, Rabi. Take a swing," Sammy goaded. "I want to watch you spin around again." He gave me another push. "What you got, red dot? Let's see that pretty twirl you do."

Parents were starting to stand up in the bleachers, trying to see what was going on between us, but they were too far away to help. Sammy gave me another shove. "Why don't you swing, twirly? Let's see your swing."

Miguel grabbed my bat off the ground. "I'll take a swing."

That got everyone's attention. Sammy took a step back, and I swear he looked scared. Joe gave a whoop of glee.

"Oh yeah! Now it's a *fight*!"

I grabbed the bat away from Miguel. "Are you crazy?"

"Someone's got to shut him up," Miguel said.

11

Mr. Cocoran came busting in between us as I turned around to glare at Sammy.

"What's going on here?" Mr. Cocoran shouted.

Sammy pointed at us. "They were going to hit me with that bat!"

"That's not what hap—" I started to say, but Mr. Cocoran shut me down.

"Cool it, Jones! I don't take shift time off from Milrow just so I can watch you pick fights on this team. Especially not after you lose a game."

"I didn't pick—"

"Is that a baseball bat in your hand?"

"Uh…"

Sammy was grinning at me from behind Cocoran's back.

"What are you thinking, Jones? You don't pick fights with your own team. And you sure as heck don't threaten another human being with a bat."

"Sammy's human?" Joe asked. "You sure about that?"

Mr. Cocoran swung around. "Save the smart remarks, mister. One more, and you're off this team."

I tried again. "I didn't pick the fight—"

But Mr. Cocoran was all wound up now. "Not another word, Jones. You're an inch from being kicked off this team yourself. You snark from the bench and you pick fights after you lose games. That's not good sports-manship, not by a long shot."

I could tell Mr. Cocoran was going to go on, but someone honked a horn from the parking lot.

He glared at us all, looking from Sammy and Travis and Rob and Bill, to me, to Miguel and Joe. Parents were coming down onto the field now to see what was hap-pening, including my mom and Sammy's parents. The car honked again. "You're lucky I've got to get to my shift," Mr. Cocoran said. "But we'll talk about this next practice. Don't think we're done here. Now clear out, all of you."

My mom came up behind me in her yellow sari. "Rabi, what's going on? Were you fighting?"

"It wasn't anything, Mom. Just some joking around."

"It didn't look like joking."

As everyone else left the field and walked up the low grassy slope to the parking lot, Sammy looked back at me one more time, making a face at my mom's back.

Red dot, he mouthed.

I was so mad, I could have gone after him right then and there. But Mr. Cocoran was watching me, and I could tell he was just waiting for me to step out of line.

"Rabi?" my mom pressed, not seeing what was hap-pening behind her.

"It's nothing, Mom."

I glared after Sammy, wishing he were dead. Hating Mr. Cocoran for taking Sammy's side. Hating them all.

I feel bad about it now, looking back.

When you're mad, you wish all kinds of things on people. Maybe you even think they deserve it. But it turns out that I didn't want anyone dead. I didn't even want anyone hurt.

Not even when Mr. Cocoran tried to eat my brains.

CHAPTER 2

But I'm getting ahead of myself. Mr. Cocoran didn't try to snack on my skull candy right away. I mean, he hated me right from the moment when I started asking questions about his baseball strategies, but that's not a brain-eating offense, right? It takes some serious weirdness to turn your baseball coach into a flesh-hungry maniac.

After the baseball game, I was going to stay behind with Miguel and Joe to practice batting, because no matter how crummy Mr. Cocoran was as a coach, I really had lost the game for my team. I had to be honest about that: I needed serious batting help.

My mom says that if you want to get good at anything, you have to practice at it, and practice really hard, otherwise you don't deserve to have anything at all. She speaks four languages—Hindi, Bengali, English, and French—because she practices. She likes to remind me about how my grandpa (my *dadu*, in Bengali) walked out of Bangladesh and into India with nothing to his name. Just a poor farmer who couldn't read or write or even do math, but he was crazy determined, and he taught himself all those things. Eventually he worked his way up until he was the finest sari merchant in Kolkata, taking custom orders for saris that had diamonds and gold woven into them for some of Bollywood's biggest stars. But he sweated it all the way.

So I knew that if I really wanted something, I had to be willing to sweat for it. And even if it was 102 degrees, I was willing to sweat for baseball, and Miguel and Joe were willing to help.

The problem was that Sammy and his friends decided to hang around the baseball field, too, looking to finish what Sammy had started. They were watching us from the bleachers, passing a cigarette back and forth among them, acting all tough. Now that everyone else was gone, they were starting to call us names.

"Looks like we're going to get that fight after all," Joe said. He didn't sound scared. Mostly just curious about what would happen next.

Just so you know, Joe is kind of crazy. His dad drinks a lot of beer and gets in a lot of fights, and the two things Joe seems to have learned from that are that he's never going to drink alcohol and that nothing is as scary as his dad—so Joe does whatever he wants, and doesn't worry much about the consequences. He's always wearing raggedy clothes, and he cuts his blond hair with clippers without using a mirror, so it always sticks up in chunks. He thinks everything is a joke.

Sammy took a drag on his cigarette and stood up. He pointed at me, real serious, like, *You're dead.* His buddies all stood up, too. One of them had to be six feet tall. Rob Ziegler had been held back for, like, three grades.

"They're going to turn us into mango pulp," I said.

"Doesn't your mom make that?" Joe asked.

"You're thinking of *aamar payesh*," I said.

"Oh yeah," Joe said. "I love that stuff. I could totally go for that right now."

We were about to get pounded, and Joe was thinking about mango rice pudding. Like I said, Joe's kind of crazy. My mom got really worried when I started hanging out with him, because she was sure it was the first step to me not going to college and not getting my engineering degree, which basically is the worst thing you can do to your mom if she's a mom like mine.

I grabbed Joe's and Miguel's arms. "Let's go to Milrow Park," I suggested. "They won't bother us there."

"That's because it smells like dead dogs out there," Joe said.

"You seriously going to let these idiots run us off?" Miguel asked, looking hard at Sammy.

Miguel won't back down from anyone who acts like a jerk. He's like a samurai from ancient Japan that way. If he thinks something's not right, he doesn't back down, no matter what.

Which is just how his dad used to be, too, and it didn't do him any good at all. The apple didn't fall far from the tree with Miguel. His dad made all kinds of trouble out at Milrow's meatpacking plant. Even made a video of what it was like working inside the place and uploaded it to YouTube. He was crazy brave, like Miguel, but it ruined his whole family.

Now I was afraid we were getting to that point with Miguel, where it didn't matter how bad the odds were—Miguel would step up and fight, just because it wasn't right to back down.

"They're not running us off," I said. "It's just being smart about the stats. You might be strong, and Joe might be crazy—"

"I like to think of myself as inspired," Joe said.

"—but they're all bigger than us. Even you, Miguel. And six against three doesn't add up to anything other than a bloodbath."

"You can't live afraid," Miguel said.

"I can't live dead, either, so *come on*."

"You ever stop to think maybe we could win?" Miguel asked.

"Yeah," Joe said. "Like in X-Men. When the odds are against you, and you really step up."

"Quit with the comic book stuff," I said. "You're both nuts."

"You sure it won't smell at Milrow?" Miguel asked.

I wasn't, but I wasn't going to tell them that.

"Oh yeah. It'll be totally fine."

CHAPTER 3

"It smells like dead dogs, Rabi."

Miguel laughed at Joe's wrinkled nose of disgust. "You didn't actually believe him, did you?"

"It's not that bad," I said, trying to make the best of it. "At least we're not downwind of the feedlots."

We were sitting on our bikes, staring at the Milrow beef-processing facility, a whole series of big white metal-sided buildings and smokestacks puffing steam. A giant Milrow cow logo smiled out at us from the side of the nearest building, along with the words MILROW MEAT SOLUTIONS—MODERN FARMING EXCELLENCE MEETS ALL-NATURAL QUALITY.

Beyond that, it was feedlots to the horizon, an ocean of cows all packed together, practically knee-deep in their own manure, feeding in long troughs full of whatever it was that Milrow gave its cows to fatten them up.

We were told in school that Milrow makes beef to feed people in seven states, but until you see cows and feedlots as far as the eye can see, you can't really understand how big a deal that is. Acres and acres of cows, all waiting to go in one end of the plant as mooing animals, and pop out the other end as cuts of beef that would get packed into refrigerated trucks, where they'd be taken to supermarkets all over.

"Whew," Joe said, covering his nose with his shirt. "I'll sure be glad when they're all steak instead of stink."

I had to agree there. My family doesn't eat beef, because my mom's Hindu, but looking at all those sad, packed-together cows, it seemed like they'd sure be better off once they were turned into chunks of shrink-wrapped steak instead of a bunch of mangy and gross animals spattered with manure.

When I thought about it, though, it was kind of disgusting that this was where all that bright, clean-looking supermarket meat was coming from.

A big old semitruck was coming up the road, packed with more cows for the feedlots. We rolled our bikes out of the way as it rushed past in a blast of smelly wind and dust and loud mooing from inside the metal trailer. We all gagged from the stink.

"Come on," I said. "Let's go hit some balls before we get run over."

"It's going to be just as nasty on the grass."

"Look at it," I said. "It's a nice park."

Milrow Park stood just a little way off from the processing plant, and it really was nice. Emerald-green grass, perfectly manicured, with picnic tables and clumps of trees scattered around for shade. Of course, it was also a ghost park, because feedlots and a meatpacking plant don't make for a great view at your average Sunday family barbecue and touch football game.

My dad said Milrow only made the park because it had to clean up a huge sewer lagoon from its feedlots. There was some kind of tax deduction for turning a big lake of cow poop into a park, so they made Milrow Park and called it open space. At first, all the trees and grass died, but they'd finally figured out how to make things grow, and now, if you held your nose and just focused on the park, it was actually pretty nice—that is, if you'd run out of all other options.

"If you want to complain, go ahead," I said. "This is the only place where Sammy and his thugs aren't going to bother us. Better get used to it."

"I'm getting sick and tired of Sammy pushing us around," Miguel said. He was looking at the meatpacking plant as he said it, but I knew he was thinking about his mom and dad. And if he was thinking about his mom and dad, that meant he was thinking about Sammy's dad, too—the guy who ran Milrow Meats, and who had probably been the person to go after Miguel's family after Miguel's dad posted the meatpacking video on YouTube.

"Just be glad you were born here in America," I said. "Otherwise, they might have gone after you, too."

"Milrow doesn't care about me. Just people who make trouble in there. They don't bother us when we're being cheap, quiet workers, but as soon as you stand up…Bam!" Miguel drove his fist into his palm. "They bounce us right out of the country."

"You don't know for sure that's what happened," Joe said.

"My dad made that video of the plant, and the next day, ICE raided. That wasn't a coincidence. That was Sammy's dad, sweeping out noisy workers."

"Yeah," said Joe, "but still, your dad *was* illegal. He was breaking the law. It was bound to happen sometime."

"Nobody at Milrow cared about that before," Miguel said. "He worked there for fifteen years. But as soon as he started saying the line was getting sped up too much and that people were getting hurt, suddenly he's a troublemaker. And next thing you know, Milrow sics ICE on my family.

23

There're still tons of people working in there who don't have passports or green cards or anything, and Milrow doesn't mind them. Just my dad and my mom. Milrow threw them away like garbage."

I didn't know what to say. For sure, Miguel's dad had been making trouble at Milrow, and for sure, he and Miguel's mom were both illegal immigrants, so when the department of Immigration and Customs Enforcement raided, they hadn't stood a chance. They'd gotten swept up and thrown into detention, then thrown out of the country. Miguel ended up living with his aunt and uncle—who hadn't been making trouble at the plant, and hadn't been raided.

"Well," Joe said, "at least you're a citizen. At least they can't deport you."

Miguel shook his head. "You never know with ICE. Sometimes they don't seem so picky. If they get my aunt and uncle, what happens to me then? Foster home? Or maybe ICE dumps me over the border, too, 'cause I got no family here."

"Forget that!" Joe said. "If you needed a place to live, you'd live with me."

"With your dad?" I said. "No way. Miguel would live with me."

"No. He'd live with me. I've got the comic books."

24

"Yeah, well, my mom makes all the good food," I said.

"TV dinners are great!" Joe said.

"How come you're always sniffing around my house at dinnertime, then?"

"I'm just trying to be nice. Miguel eats meat. All you vegetarians eat are nuts and berries."

"We're not vegetarians," I said. "We eat chicken and fish. And you know it, because you stuff yourself every time you come over."

"Yeah? Well, my house is the one with the bacon." Joe grinned. "Bacon and comics. You can't beat that. Baaaaa-con. MMMMMMmmm."

Miguel started to laugh. "You guys are both crazy. If I had to pick, I'd take Rabi's mom's cooking and your comics." He seemed to have shaken off his funk, though. "Come on. Let's go play some ball," he said.

We went out onto the park's green grass and started practicing, with Joe pitching and Miguel helping me with my swing. After a while, we barely even noticed the smell coming from the feedlots or the mooing of the cows.

Miguel watched me swing and miss.

Swing and miss.

Swing and foul one off.

Swing and miss.

"You always tense up at the plate," Miguel said. "You got to stay loose."

"Yeah, well, there's a ball flying at me," I said. "Of course I tense up."

"No. There's a ball flying *past* you."

Joe laughed at that. "Except that one time, remember? When Rabi got beaned in the head? He fell right over. Just like in a cartoon."

Joe pretended to be me, splatting on the grass, his arms and legs spread out in a big *X*, and his tongue sticking out of the side of his mouth, like he was unconscious.

"We're supposed to be building up his confidence," Miguel reminded him.

Joe opened his eyes and sat up. "Come on, you got to admit it was funny." He fell back and threw out his arms again. "SPLAT!"

"Aaanyway," Miguel said, making a big thing about ignoring Joe, "that's why you got the batting helmet, right? It's armor. Just like with Iron Man in Joe's comics. You got to think like you're armored, like you're a baseball-killing machine."

"You ready or not?" Joe called.

I nodded. *Baseball-killing machine*, I thought. Not

afraid of the ball, or how fast it was going, just hunting for it, wanting it—

Joe whipped a fast one at me.

WHACK!

I totally got a piece of it. The ball blasted across the field, fast and low. It bounced and bounced and then rolled into the shade under a couple of trees that Milrow had planted.

Miguel and Joe both cheered. "Nice shot!" Joe said.

"Would have been a hit, for sure."

Miguel declared it was good to end on a high note, so after that we just started throwing the ball around and talking.

Joe told us about a new stack of comic books that he'd ordered using his mom's credit card when she wasn't looking, and he was supposed to get delivery in a couple of days.

"I just hope she's not home when the package shows up. If I'm there for UPS, she'll never even know."

"You're going to get busted," Miguel said.

"Nah." Joe hucked the ball, fast and hard, to me. "She orders tons of junk on Amazon all the time. I already deleted the receipt from her e-mail, so she might not even notice it's on her card with all those other charges."

I sent the ball to Miguel, and Miguel fired it off to Joe. *Thwock*, solid in his glove.

"So what did you get?" I asked.

"X-Men, and a new Spider-Man, and I got another Transmetropolitan."

I perked up at that. Transmetropolitan is this crazy comic about a journalist named Spider Jerusalem who lives in the future and investigates all these stories about corruption. He's kind of burned-out, so it's not really, you know, good role-model stuff. When my mom caught me with it, she gave me a big lecture about drugs and drinking and violence and girls and all the other things in the comic, and how these things weren't supposed to be glorified. Then she threw the comic away.

I didn't mind, really, because I knew she meant well, but all she would have had to do was point at Joe's dad if she wanted to talk about what drinking or drugs got you, because walking into that guy's house when he was drunk was scary enough that you never wanted to drink, ever.

To me at least, Spider Jerusalem's craziness never seemed like the point of the comic. The point was that the guy was always trying to fight the good fight and uncover corruption, even though everyone around him was too lazy or greedy or stupid to care. Kind of like Miguel, or even Miguel's dad, when he stood up for things and got socked for it. It was that whole samurai thing: too much honor to sit and lie low. Spider Jerusalem kept on fighting anyway.

Also, Spider Jerusalem had a cat with two faces, and he ate things like takeout monkey burgers and cartons of caribou eyeballs for breakfast.

How cool is that?

So anyway, I wasn't allowed to have those comics at my house, but Joe's mom hardly paid attention, and if we avoided his dad, we could go over to Joe's and read them there.

We kept chucking the baseball and talking about nothing in particular. And I think that's the most important thing: We were doing something that felt so normal, and at the same time, everything around us was already starting to get weird. Things were normal…and then they weren't.

"What's that smell?" Joe asked.

Miguel and I sniffed. *Nasty.* "Is that the feedlots?"

"I think it's coming from Milrow." I gagged.

"Whoa!" Miguel said. "That's just wrong."

The smell was definitely coming out of the meatpacking plant, and it was bad.

But telling you the smell was bad is a complete understatement. It smelled like a combination of cow manure and rotten meat.

Even that doesn't describe it, because, basically, manure and rotting meat is what Milrow smells like a lot of the time—it's disgusting, but it's totally normal.

This was worse.

Bucket-of-puke-that-you-left-out-in-the-sun-and-then-poured-over-hot-coals worse. Ashy-barfy-rotten-meat-dead-cow-manure-sewer nasty.

"Oh my god!" We were all gagging. "What is it?"

Joe retched. "I thought you said it wouldn't stink out here, Rabi!"

I was covering my mouth with my T-shirt. "It never smells like *this*."

We all started for our bikes, holding our shirts over our noses, covering our faces with our baseball gloves. Anything to cut the stench.

"Agh! It's killing me!" Miguel said.

As we climbed onto our bikes, we suddenly saw a bunch of workers scrambling out of the meatpacking plant. I saw Miguel's uncle and aunt and a whole bunch of the other Mexican workers all piling out the door and running for the parking lots.

A siren started going off, and more people came pouring outside.

Miguel's uncle caught sight of us staring at the commotion. He changed direction and hurried over.

"What are you *niños* doing here?" He was holding a blood-covered apron over his face. Cow blood, I guessed. He hadn't even changed out of his work clothes before he ran out of there.

"We were just playing baseball."

Mr. Castillo glanced back at the plant. I swear he looked frightened. "You shouldn't be here. Go play by your school."

"Why?"

I mean, it was pretty obvious why. The whole place smelled like rot-poop-dead-cow-puke—but, you know, other than that.

Mr. Castillo just shook his head and didn't answer. "You shouldn't be out here. This air is very bad. *Muy malo. Muy muy malo.*"

"Why's everyone running?" Miguel asked. "What smells so bad?"

But Miguel's uncle wouldn't say. He just made urgent shooing motions at us like we were a bunch of chickens or something.

"*¡No más preguntas!* Just go on! *¡Váyanse!*" he said, and he looked so serious, we didn't dare to ask any more questions. We stood on our pedals and got out of there.

But this smell wasn't like other smells. It didn't get better as we pedaled for town; it chased us the whole way, making our eyes tear up and making us cough and gag.

It was the kind of stink that made you want to hunker down under a blanket to keep the air out. It made you want to duct-tape the windows closed and hold your breath, praying the smell would just pass you by—because, if you were honest about the thing that was billowing over the cornfields and chasing us back to town, there was only one name that fit:

Pure Evil.

CHAPTER 4

Mom opened the door ahead of me, making a face at the outside air. "Where have you been, *khoka*?"

"We were at the park. Over by Milrow."

"Is that where this smell is coming from?"

I was gagging as I ducked inside. "Yeah."

Mom shut the door quickly, but the smell followed me in. We turned up the AC to try to filter it out, but it didn't help.

"Go take a shower," she said. "You smell."

"It's not me! It's the air."

But she wouldn't listen. "Go clean up."

I went and took a long shower and soaped myself three times. Even after that, I kept smelling the stink, but I couldn't decide if it was actually still on me, or if it was bad air sneaking into the house, or if it was just my mind going crazy. When the water turned cold, I gave up scrubbing.

By the time I came downstairs, the stink was being replaced by other smells: cumin and coriander and mustard seeds frying as Mom started to work on dinner.

"Rabi," my mom said, looking up from the stove. "What was it that happened after your baseball game? It looked like you were in a fight with that other boy. The Riggoni boy."

"It was just kid stuff. He doesn't like that I can't hit."

"You can hit. I've seen you."

"No, Mom. I can't. I suck."

"Don't use that word."

"It's not a curse word. Vacuums suck."

My mom said something in Bengali under her breath. "My son thinks he is so clever." To me, she said, "The word is the word, and we both know it's not nice."

"Yeah, well, Sammy calls me 'red dot.' I guess that's not nice, either."

I went into the living room and turned on the TV, started flipping channels. My mom shut off the stove and followed me in.

"Do your other classmates say these things, too?" She

stood in front of me, blocking my view, a whole wall of yellow sari.

"Nah. It's just Sammy. He's a jerk. He probably went to Chicago and learned it from some of his jerk friends. There's no way he came up with it on his own. He's not smart enough."

Which was true, because, let's face it, if you're Indian and you live in the middle of nowhere, nobody knows how to stereotype you. Half the people in America can't even find India on a map, let alone know what the culture's like. You might think I'm joking, but I'm serious: Unless I'm in a big city, if I tell people I'm half Indian, they usually think I'm talking about Native Americans—Sioux or Arapaho, people like that. They definitely aren't thinking Bengali.

And what confuses people even more is that my dad's white. Or, if you want to get all specific, he's German/Swedish/Scottish, with maybe some Polish. Born and raised in Delbe, just like me. So I'm like a third-generation Bengali/German/Swedish/Scottish-with-maybe-Polish, Delbe Iowan. One hundred percent mutt, I like to say. My dad says that actually means I'm 100 percent American.

"Has Sammy been saying this long?" my mom asked.

I started to answer, but I caught a glimpse of the TV

and was surprised to see Sammy's dad staring out at me from the screen. It was almost like I'd summoned Mr. Riggoni by talking about his kid. "Uhh…" I leaned to the side so I could see around Mom to the TV.

"Rabi?"

I tore my eyes from the TV. "No, Mom. He just learned it. He'll probably forget it tomorrow and go back to picking on someone else. It's nothing. He's a jerk." I pointed at the TV. "Look. They're talking about Milrow."

Mom turned around and we both watched. "That's Sammy's father, yes?"

"Yeah," I said, thinking about what the guy had done to Miguel's mom and dad. "He's a jerk, too. It runs in the family." I turned up the volume.

"Why do you say so?" Mom asked, and I realized I'd probably said too much. She didn't know that most of Miguel's family was here illegally.

"It's nothing," I said, and hit the volume up another couple notches. "Can I watch this?"

Mom finally moved clear so that we could both see. Sammy's dad was standing in front of the Milrow plant with a reporter.

He was saying, "…Retrofitting for the processing systems will take no more than a few days. Obviously, when we open closed systems like this, there are some local impacts—"

"You mean the air—" the reporter started, but Mr. Riggoni overrode her.

"—is completely safe." He took a deep breath, which I thought was pretty heroic considering how nasty I knew it was out there.

"Entirely safe. We're overseen by both the USDA and the EPA, and we take our obligations seriously. Milrow Meats is entirely in compliance with relevant environmental regulations. Any impacts should be entirely gone by nightfall."

The reporter looked like she was fighting not to gag, but she managed to make herself smile and turn back to the studio. The news anchors all smiled as well and turned to face the camera. "That's right, folks. Just keep your windows closed for another hour or two, and things should clear up."

It was weird, looking at the anchors in their news studio and the lady reporter behind them on the screen, everyone smiling along with Sammy's dad. Everyone pretending that the air outside wasn't foul and that Mr. Riggoni wasn't full of it.

"They're lying," I said. "This smell wasn't planned. No way."

"Don't be silly, *khoka*."

"I was *there*. All the workers were running away. Miguel's uncle told us to run, too."

"Don't make up stories."

"I'm not! There were sirens and everyone was running out of that place like they expected it to explode."

Mom still gave me her best *I don't believe you* look.

"Okay," I said, backtracking. "Maybe it wasn't going to explode. But Miguel's uncle looked *scared*. Sammy's dad is a total liar."

"You're just saying this because you're angry at Sammy."

"I'm saying it because it's true! Sammy's a total jerk, and his dad's a liar. That guy would do anything for money. Lying's nothing to him."

"How do you know?"

I bit my tongue. I didn't want to go into that. Miguel didn't like having people talk about his family situation; he'd only told me and Joe about his parents' immigration status because we were best friends. And he'd sworn us to secrecy.

"I just do."

Mom looked at me a moment longer. "Don't make up stories, Rabi. Mr. Riggoni is very respected." I could tell she was disappointed in me as she turned and went back into the kitchen. "No more stories, *khoka*. Come and help me make the *papad* and set the table for dinner."

I nodded, but I didn't get up right away. I just couldn't take my eyes off the TV with its smiling news announcers. It was like he'd hypnotized them or something. He was covering everything up, and he was getting away with it. He made lots of money and looked real good in a suit, so everyone trusted him—even when he was lying out of both sides of his mouth.

Even my mom trusted the guy. She was already laying chunks of fish into the simmering spices of her *macher jhol*, ready to go back to regular life. She believed every word he'd said, because he was "respected."

Why wasn't anyone challenging him? The newspeople weren't saying anything. The workers weren't saying anything, even though they'd all been running away, too. It was like all the grown-ups had decided not to tell the truth, or even bother to look at it.

The TV news switched over to some story about Homeland Security, breaking the spell. I wasn't sure exactly what needed to be done about Sammy's lying dad, but I was starting to think the answer lay in Joe's comic books.

Good old Spider Jerusalem was practically screaming at me, telling me what he'd do if he saw some lying fat cat like that, right on the news.

Spider Jerusalem would have stuffed himself on caribou eyeballs, and then he would have gone out and investigated.

CHAPTER 5

Unfortunately, Spider Jerusalem didn't have a mom and a bunch of family back in India. My whole plan to go poke around Milrow got derailed by real life.

In the middle of the night, my mom got a call from India.

India calls only at oddball times of the night because they're on the other side of the world when it's daytime for them, and when they call, it's only for three reasons:

1) A wedding
2) A new baby
3) Someone died

I was pretty sure no one over there was getting married, because the next cousin I had who was going to get an arranged marriage was fourteen, so he had a while to wait yet. And the next in line after that was Mishtu, and she was twelve. And none of my already-married cousins had any babies on the way.

I got a cold, sick feeling in my stomach.

Mom was talking fast on the phone in Bengali, and a couple minutes later she came in and said, "Rabi, there's been an accident in Kolkata family. *Mashima* has been in a car crash."

Mashima—that could have been any one of my mother's five sisters. My mom seemed to read my mind. "Dhira Mashima," she supplied.

It was still hard to remember which one she was; they were all a blur of saris and older ladies who sometimes gave me candy or rupees for gifts. I searched my mind and finally placed her. She was the second-oldest sister, with a big smile and who used to give me chocolate when we visited her flat.

She basically only spoke Bengali, so there wasn't a whole lot I could really know about her, unless my mom or one of Dhira Mashima's kids was around to translate into English. Mostly she would just smile at me, and I'd smile back, and then the silence between us would stretch and stretch until I had to leave the room because

I couldn't take not actually being able to say anything except "hi" and "how are you?"

"Is she okay?"

"We're not sure. She's in the hospital. I'm going to make tickets to fly tomorrow, if we can find seats."

I was still trying to get the sleep out of my eyes, but Mom was bustling around, talking about tickets and driving to Chicago, and who she could get to come over and take care of the yard.

"Mom?"

"Yes, *khoka*?"

"Do I have to go, too?"

Mom turned and looked at me, shocked. "Of course you have to go. She's your *mashima*. Your family needs you."

"But…" I kind of understood what she meant about family, but really, what good was I going to do over there? My mom was the kind of take-charge person who could push around hospital doctors and nurses. She could probably help, but me?

"Won't I just be in the way?" I asked.

"It's important to show you care. You must come."

Spider Jerusalem didn't have to deal with stuff like this. I didn't want to be a jerk, but how was I going to figure out what Sammy's dad had been lying about if I was in India?

43

After the news report on the TV, I'd called Miguel and Joe. They'd both seen the news, too.

"Total liar," Joe pronounced. "Full-on Magneto evil liar."

"Yeah," Miguel said. "My uncle saw that, too. He said it was bogus."

"So what's the scoop?" I asked.

"It's gonna chill your blood."

"Yeah???"

But Miguel wouldn't say any more. So all night I'd been lying in bed, waiting for daybreak so that I could go over and shake the story out of him.

And now India was calling.

Saying that I didn't want to go wouldn't do any good. I needed a different plan. Appeal to family and duty.

"If I'm over there, I'll just be in your way," I said. "I can't speak much Bengali, and everyone's going to be busy. But if I stay here, then you'd be free to go to the hospital and help Dhira Mashima. I'd be fine. I don't mind. I just don't want to be in the way when you need to be taking care of your sister."

Mom looked doubtful. "But where would you stay?"

"I could stay with Miguel."

"Don't be silly. You can't just impose on his family like that. I could be gone a week. More, maybe."

"They wouldn't mind—" I almost said, *They're working so hard they're hardly around the house at all*, but that wasn't a good thing to tell your mom, so instead I said, "They like having kids around. It wouldn't bother them. They love kids."

"That must be why they're taking care of Miguel while his parents are looking for work in California."

That was the story we'd been telling everyone about where Miguel's parents had gone. "Yeah. They really like kids," I said, nodding vigorously. "Love 'em."

"All right," she said, doubtfully. "I can call them. But no guarantees."

By morning, Mr. and Mrs. Castillo had agreed to let me stay, and I was packing a bag to stay at Miguel's. I felt a little guilty for misleading my mom, but it was for a good cause, I figured. Now, as I zipped up my duffel and slung it over my shoulder, I couldn't wait to get the inside scoop from Mr. Castillo about what had really happened at Milrow Meat Solutions.

Spider Jerusalem was on the trail of a scandal, and he wasn't going to let up until all the rotten corruption had been brought to light.

CHAPTER 6

To be honest, Miguel's house wasn't my favorite place in the world.

Mr. and Mrs. Castillo were nice people, but they also really did work all the time, because Milrow didn't pay much. Half the time they were working crazy shifts at Milrow, and the other half, they were doing other odd jobs and work. Miguel had to do a lot of the cooking and clean up the dishes and do laundry for himself. And on top of that, Miguel had a job where he'd go out and mow lawns so he could help contribute to getting his folks back across the border.

Mrs. Castillo would sometimes try to take care of us, and she'd do cool things like let us drink *café de olla*, a kind of coffee that has cinnamon in it and a ton of sugar.

But it wasn't like my house, where you could just hit up your mom for a snack of mango pickle and rice; at Miguel's you had to go dig in the fridge and hope that you didn't also have to go to the grocery store, and if you did, you had to hope that someone had the cash to do it.

I ended up helping with a lot of the housework, too, because if you're going to freeload at someone's house, it's what you do. I did dishes, helped Miguel mow lawns, chopped vegetables for dinner, whatever needed doing.

But you know what? It was all worth it, because Mr. and Mrs. Castillo had a story to tell, all right, and I would have worked twice as hard to hear what they had to say the first day I got there.

We had just finished dinner, and Miguel and I were washing the dishes by hand because they didn't have a dishwasher. Miguel kept giving dishes back to me to scrub twice.

"Do it again," he said.

"I already did."

"Feel that." He rubbed his finger on the plate. "You got to get the oil off, too, not just the food. I thought Indians knew how to work."

"I'm only half Indian."

"Half Indian, but pure momma's boy."

I got more soap on my sponge and did it again, while

Miguel watched me like a hawk. Behind us, Mr. Castillo was practically asleep at the table, after finishing a brutal shift, but Mrs. Castillo was wiping down counters and putting everything back in order.

Finally, I couldn't hold back anymore. "So?" I elbowed Miguel. "What happened at the plant? You said you were going to tell me."

In a single second, the kitchen went from happy and relaxed to dead silent. Mr. Castillo, who I'd thought had been dozing, was suddenly looking at Miguel, his brow knitted.

"You told him?" Mr. Castillo asked.

Miguel looked down. I'd never seen him look embarrassed before. In school or on the baseball field, he was always a rock. But when Mr. Castillo looked hard at him, he seemed to shrink.

Mrs. Castillo was looking from her husband to her nephew, her warmth and friendliness gone entirely. "What are you thinking?" she asked.

And then she turned to Spanish. She aimed rapid-fire words of authority at Miguel, her hand chopping the air for emphasis. I caught *mamá* and *papá*, but the rest of it went by in a blur. Her expression was hard and disappointed. She finished up with "*¡Muy peligroso!*" and a final chop of the hand.

I'd always thought of Mrs. Castillo as a pretty quiet woman, a nice lady who always smiled at me, even after a long day at work. But she didn't look that way now. I wouldn't have crossed her, not in a million years, looking like that.

But Miguel turned stubborn under her words. "He's my friend," he said, and the way he said it, he looked just like he did when he was about to go out and try to beat up some bully, even though he was outnumbered. Straightening up, all determination. "He's my *best* friend."

I looked from Mr. and Mrs. Castillo to Miguel, feeling like I was in the middle of a standoff, and something terrible was at stake.

"I won't tell anyone," I said. "I can keep a secret."

Mr. Castillo frowned at me. "Good secrets are kept by telling no one at all."

"I know you're here illegally," I said. "I haven't told anyone about that. You can trust me. I didn't even tell my parents that Miguel's mom and dad got grabbed by ICE. I don't tell secrets."

"Secrets." Miguel's uncle laughed sharply. "Yes. Secrets. If you know half the things that happen in Milrow..." he trailed off. "You know nothing. You know less than zero."

"I know something went wrong out at the meatpacking plant. And I know Sammy's dad is a liar."

"That man…" Mr. Castillo made a face of disgust. He seemed to make a decision. "That man would do anything for Milrow. They want money, money, money. All they want is for workers to work harder. *Más duro, más duro, más duro.* Always it is *más duro.* They do not care if people are hurt, because there are always more people from Mexico or Honduras or Ecuador. I have seen people lose arms and legs and fingers in that place. In those machines. Those fast knives…" He trailed off. "It is a sickness in that place. They care about nothing except making a little more money. And now they feed their cows strange things to make them grow faster. They give them drugs to make them not die when they live in dirt and filth. They use the feathers and droppings and bits of chickens from their chicken factories and grind them up and give them to their cows for food, because it is cheap to feed their cows the trash of other places.…I see all of this, and I do not complain, because they will deport me like *that.*" He snapped his fingers.

"But now, I tell you, these Milrow men in their fine suits, and their scientists in their clean white lab coats, they are doing new things.…They are finding new drugs to make the meat taste better, to make it grow fat, and these drugs…these things that they feed them…they make the cows strange. The animals do not act as they should, and their meat does not smell as it should, and when you cut them, they do not bleed and die as they should—"

"Raúl," Mrs. Castillo said. "You frighten them. You do not see such things."

"I have eyes," he said stubbornly. "I see the cows when they come into the line to be killed by my hand. I see how they stagger. They are not natural. Something was always wrong with the cows, because so many were sick and fed on bad things, but now it is getting worse.

"I think something is changing out there in the feed-lots. All those cows packed together, fattening on strange things, and sick near to death. These cows are not cows as I knew them when I was a boy and worked on my father's ranch in Tamaulipas. It is not the same. These cows are not cows."

"Of course they are cows," Mrs. Castillo said. "You're telling the boys ghost stories now."

But Mr. Castillo shook his head stubbornly. "No, Nina. Something is different. It is changing."

CHAPTER 7

I spent the night with strange dreams, and all of them were about cows.

Cows from India like I used to see when we went over to visit family. White cows with high humps on their backs and garlands of marigolds on their short horns, people feeding them grass and getting blessings from the priest who cared for them. A sacred act. And then others: cows in feedlot trucks blasting past us on the highway as we pedaled our bikes out to Milrow Meat Solutions, their furry faces pressed against the grates of the truck trailers, the animals mooing with panic and stinking with manure as they disappeared into the darkness of the plant.

And then other dreams—weirder ones. Steaks that talked to me and asked me for directions back to their ranch. Cafeteria hamburgers that jumped off school lunch trays and dashed for the doors, with all us kids chasing after them. I kept saying, "But I don't even eat cow!" as I grabbed at bacon double cheeseburgers that hopped around like grasshoppers, and dove for sliders that were zipping down hallways and dodging us like feral cats.

I woke to Miguel shaking me.

"What?" I mumbled groggily. I was covered with sweat and felt like I hadn't slept at all.

"Time to work," Miguel said.

I groaned, but dragged myself out of bed and let Miguel prod me out into the sweat of the summer to mow lawns.

Miguel had a Weedwacker and a beat-up gas mower, so I'd do the mowing while he did all the careful edge-trimming work, and if we got the work done fast enough, we would be free until baseball practice and the humiliations of Mr. Cocoran.

Neither of us could have guessed that the world was about to fall apart.

"Hey, Miguel?" I said as we shoved the mower over the curb and rattled down Poplar Street on the way to Miguel's next job. "You think your uncle's right about the cows at Milrow being unnatural?"

Miguel shrugged. "My uncle's always telling stories.

All about the *chupacabra* coming to suck the blood out of goats. Things like that. He likes to tell ghost stories."

"But you don't think he's doing that now, do you? Mr. Riggoni was totally lying. We know that. And that smell was all kinds of wrong."

Miguel shushed me suddenly. I realized where we were.

The big old house before us had, like, an acre of grass around it.

"Seriously? You do their lawn?"

We were staring up at Sammy Riggoni's house.

"It's money," Miguel said.

"But his dad's the guy who got your mom and dad—"

Miguel cut me off with a hard look. "I don't got the luxury of being all prissy about where my money comes from."

"Sorry. Okay." But it seemed so wrong.

I'd never guessed that Miguel would have to work for the people he hated most in the world.

I guess that's what not having money does. It takes away choices. The people with the cash get to make the decisions, and you just got to swallow your pride.

But then, to add insult to injury, Sammy came out the front door, sucking on a lemonade and smiling like he was getting the biggest, bestest Christmas present ever. He plopped into a chair with a stack of comics and started reading, looking up at us every once in a while with a nasty smirk.

"Ignore him," Miguel said.

We started working, sweating it out in the humidity and heat. I pushed the mower, and Miguel did the edging, and Sammy watched us work out in the sun, sitting on the shady porch, sipping that icy lemonade.

I didn't like the way he was looking at us. It was like he was planning something, and it had to be no good.

Finally Miguel got sick of it, and he shut off the Weedwacker.

"What's your problem?" Miguel asked as he unslung the Weedwacker and wiped sweat off his face.

Sammy just grinned from the porch. "You got your passport on you?"

"What's that supposed to mean?"

Sammy stood up and leaned on the porch rail, looking down on us. "You think you can just pick up a bat and say you're going to whack me?"

I suddenly remembered the other day after the baseball game—how Miguel had picked up the bat and said, "I'll take a swing," and how scared Sammy had gotten when he was faced with someone who wasn't scared of him.

Miguel looked at Sammy, hard. I expected him to step up, like he always did when he ran into a bully, but to my surprise, he didn't. He just shrugged and turned away. "Whatever, man."

"That all you got, lawn boy?" Sammy taunted.

I got in between them, hoping to draw attention away from Miguel.

"What do you mean about passports?" I asked. "Miguel's American, just like us."

"You'll see," Sammy said, grinning.

Miguel said something under his breath that sounded really bad, but he turned around and went back to pick up his Weedwacker. At first I thought Sammy didn't hear him, but then Sammy's smile turned into a scowl and he came down off the porch.

He gave Miguel a shove from behind. "Say that to my face," he challenged.

Miguel didn't even bother to look around at him. "Already did."

He started to sling the Weedwacker over his shoulder again, getting ready to pull the cord and start the engine, but Sammy grabbed him and spun him around. The Weedwacker hit the ground.

Sammy gave Miguel another shove. "Say it so I can hear it, wetback."

"Whoa!" I tried to break in. "Cut it out, Sammy. He didn't say anything!"

"Shut up, Rabi." He shoved me away. "Go back to your own country."

????????

I was so mad, I couldn't even find words. Sammy was acting like Delbe was *his* place, like I hadn't grown up here all my life, too. Like this wasn't my spot. Not mine, not Miguel's. Just his.

If he hadn't been such a big kid, I would have totally punched him in the nose, but Sammy would've creamed me. I didn't dare do it.

Miguel didn't have that problem.

Wham!

It was so fast, we all sort of stood there for a second, looking surprised that Miguel had actually punched Sammy in the face. He'd actually done it. Sammy took a step back, and his hands went up to his nose. Blood stained his fingers. Anger filled his voice. "You little..." And then he charged.

"AAAAAGGGGGhhh!"

Sammy piled into Miguel, using his size to smash him. Miguel went sprawling. Sammy landed on top and pinned Miguel's arms with his weight before starting to whale on him.

For a second, I just stood there, watching Sammy pound Miguel, amazed that we were actually fighting. It was nuts to be doing this, but we were definitely past talking. And Miguel needed help.

I dove in. I wasn't as big as Sammy or Miguel, but I had speed and momentum. I blasted into Sammy and we went tumbling across fresh-cut grass.

We all jumped to our feet at the same time. Sammy was glaring at me like he was going to rip my face off, but then Miguel came up beside me, panting. Ready for the fight.

For the first time, I realized that even if Sammy was bigger than us, Miguel and I were a team, and we had the numbers. Sammy seemed to realize the same thing, because his eyes suddenly widened. Miguel glanced at me, grinning despite a bloody lip, and I knew just what he was thinking.

We went after Sammy like a couple of wolves.

"AAAAaagghhh!"

Sammy ran toward the house, screaming for his mom. Mrs. Riggoni came out as Sammy pounded up the steps to the porch.

"What are you doing?" she shrieked. She yanked Sammy inside. "You two! Go home! Both of you! Get! Home!"

We skidded to a stop. Her face was so angry I was afraid she was about to come down and whup us herself.

I wiped my face with my arm, and blood smeared my skin. I realized I had a bloody nose. *When did I get that?*

"He started it—" I tried to say, but Miguel grabbed me and pulled me away.

"Come on, Rabi. Let it go."

I looked from Miguel to Sammy's mom, confused. Sammy was the jerk here, but now Miguel was suddenly giving up? He never gave up.

"I'm calling both of your mothers!" Mrs. Riggoni shouted as we gathered up the mower and Weedwacker. "Don't think we're not going to be talking!"

Under her gaze, coiling up electric cords and cleaning up the equipment seemed like it took forever. Now that the fight was over, I felt embarrassed. But I also felt bad about how I'd just stood there, dumb and mad and feeling scared of Sammy when he insulted me, instead of taking a swing at him, like Miguel had done. At least Miguel had stood up to him.

But now Miguel didn't look happy, either.

With Sammy's mom still shouting after us, we started home. Miguel kicked some gravel that had gotten out on the sidewalk from an ornamental garden. Just booted it.

"Stupid," he said.

"At least we made Sammy run like a chicken," I said, trying to look on the bright side.

"I'm losing that lawn for sure," Miguel said. "Twenty bucks a week, down the drain."

Now I felt really bad. I hadn't thought about the money that was supposed to help Miguel's family. "I didn't—"

"Don't worry about it," Miguel said. "He deserved it." He pushed the mower up over another curb. "But still, I'm hosed. I lose the lawn, for sure. No telling what else happens. Maybe Mr. Riggoni fires my uncle and aunt."

"Would he really do that?"

Miguel shrugged. "Who knows what white people do?"

"Cut it out. My dad wouldn't do that," I said. "He's white."

"What if I beat you up real bad, and your dad knew my aunt and uncle were illegal? What do you think he'd do then?"

I hesitated. I had no idea, really, but once again I was realizing that Miguel worried about a lot of things I just didn't need to think about. My family all had citizenship; we didn't sweat this stuff. But everyone Miguel depended on was in danger, all the time.

I couldn't help thinking of the number of times I'd

turned on the TV and caught talk-show hosts ranting about how illegal immigrants needed to be thrown out of the country. During election season, you could watch debates where politicians would all try to one-up one another on how tough they could be on immigration. States like Alabama and Arizona already wanted everyone to prove all the time that they were citizens, and if you couldn't, they'd deport you. When you added it all up, it was like there was a whole army gunning for Miguel's family. No wonder he was worried.

We made it back to Miguel's street and headed up the walk to his house.

Miguel stopped suddenly and put out his hand, holding me back.

We both stared.

His front door was wide open, swinging easy. There wasn't a single sound coming from inside.

We stood there, staring.

The white lady next door came out and saw us.

"They're gone," she said. "ICE came a couple hours ago."

Miguel's world fell out from under him.

CHAPTER 8

"You can stay with me," I said to Miguel as we walked through the empty house.

"I got to find where ICE is keeping them," Miguel said.

"Do you have a lawyer?"

I knew my mom had used an immigration lawyer when she was applying for full citizenship. Dad said the only way you got anything done when you talked to the department of immigration was if you had a good lawyer.

"I don't have money for a lawyer," Miguel said. He looked like he'd been gut-shot.

"Where'll they take them?" I asked. "Jail?"

"No. They won't go to jail. ICE has their own prisons. They could be anywhere by now." Miguel sat down on the couch, still stunned. "I don't know where they are," he said. "I don't know where any of my people are."

I pulled on Miguel's sleeve. "Come over to my house," I said. "We'll hang there. Maybe we can find someone who can help you."

"I can't pay rent for this house," Miguel said.

"It's okay, man." I grabbed him and tried to pull him up. "You can stay with me."

"What's your mom going to say?"

"Who cares? You got to stay somewhere." I looked around at the house, trying to figure out what to do.

When someone broke into your house and stole your stuff, you were supposed to call the cops. But what did you do when the cops broke in and stole your family?

"You better get all your stuff out of here," I said. "They might come back. They might come looking for you." I thought of the lady next door. "Your neighbor will probably call you in."

"Mrs. Olsen. She's a pain."

"Yeah, well, she's probably going to call someone on us. No way they're going to just let you live here alone."

"Does this mean I get put in social services?" Miguel asked. "Do I go to a foster home or something? Are they going to want my birth certificate and all that?"

I didn't know how to answer. Was he an orphan now?

Something else? All I knew was that we needed to get the heck out, and quick, before anyone Mrs. Olsen called showed up. I had a feeling that no one from the government was going to give us the help we wanted.

"Let's get your stuff," I said. "We'll hide out over at my house while we figure things out. No one's going to find you there."

"They're probably going to try to deport me, too."

"You're an American!"

"Yeah, well, my family's all in Mexico now. No one's going to want me here."

I was starting to realize how bad this was. Miguel's whole life had just gotten deleted.

"Miguel?"

He didn't answer. He was just sitting on the couch, completely shell-shocked.

It was obvious Miguel wasn't going to be able to take care of himself for a little while. He might have been able to hit triples and homers on the baseball field, and he could even make Sammy Riggoni run for his life, but this was bigger than Miguel. If he was going to get through this, he was going to need help, and that meant I needed to suck it up and figure out what to do next.

"Did your aunt and uncle have any money in the house?" I asked.

Slowly, Miguel nodded.

"Get it," I said. "Get the money, and any jewelry."

My mom was big on jewelry. Indian women kept half their money in gold and diamonds and stuff, in case anything happened. It was kind of like a bank they wore on their fingers and in their ears and on their noses and around their necks.

"Get all the valuable things," I said. "And grab any games and clothes you don't want someone else to get. We'll take it all over to my house." I pulled him up. "Come on, man. We got to hurry."

Miguel finally stood up. As he did, his expression changed. "Sammy did this. He reported them."

"We don't know that."

But I suspected Miguel was right. Sammy had been smug at his house, like he'd just kicked our butts and we didn't even know it. He'd sat on his porch, knowing what was happening down here at Miguel's house while we were away, and he'd sipped his lemonade and smiled.

Sammy had known something, all right.

"He just ruined my life," Miguel said. His hands knotted into fists. He started for the door. "I'm going to kill him."

Miguel's not crazy like Joe, but when he says he'll do something, he does it. He never chickens out and he

65

never stops. It's like when he's standing at the plate in baseball. He just stares down the pitcher, and the pitcher gets nervous because Miguel is giving him a look like, *I'm going to put this ball right back through your face.* Total focus, right?

So when Miguel said he was going to kill Sammy, I believed him.

And it scared me.

I grabbed his arm as he went past. "Whoa!" I said. "Let's get your stuff out of the house before ICE comes back." Miguel tried to jerk away, but I held on.

For a second, I was afraid Miguel was going to slug me, but I held on anyway. No way was I going to let him go after Sammy in this state. "We can deal with Sammy later," I said. "Seriously. First things first, though. We got to get out of here."

Miguel took a deep breath. Let it out slow. "Yeah. Okay."

"Good. Go get the money." A new thought came to me. "And you should get your passport, too."

Miguel nodded slowly at that. "My passport…" His expression turned to concern. He rushed into the kitchen. I heard drawers opening and slamming.

"They got my papers!" Miguel shouted. "Passport, birth certificate, everything. It's all gone!"

I felt a chill but tried to keep the worry out of my voice. "Don't sweat it," I called back. "You got to have copies somewhere, right?"

Miguel came back, shaking his head. "I don't know. I was supposed to keep that stuff safe."

"Well, we can't do anything about it now. Let's deal with your other things and get out of here. We'll figure the rest out later."

* * *

Cleaning out the house was weird because it kind of felt like we were stealing, even though we weren't. I mean, it was all Miguel's, right? It sure wasn't anyone else's. But it still felt weird. We gathered up suitcases and pillowcases filled with stuff and dragged them out into the front yard.

It was too much to carry on bikes.

"We'll get Joe," I panted, wiping sweat off my face. "Then we can get the rest."

"Wish we had a car," Miguel said.

"Yeah, well, we don't."

Miguel didn't answer. I finished tying a knot in a pillowcase and looked up.

Uh-oh.

Mr. Castillo's big maroon Ford pickup sat in the driveway. Miguel was eyeing it.

"Oh no, you don't," I said. "We can't drive! You got to know how to work the gears. It's not as easy as it looks."

"It's an automatic," Miguel said.

We both looked at each other, then back at his uncle's truck. It was just sitting there in the driveway. Big old red F-250.

Miguel started to smile.

I had the feeling things were spinning out of control.

Turns out I had no idea.

CHAPTER 9

We loaded every single thing that looked valuable into the back of the truck: all of Miguel's comic books and his baseball bat and his clothes and his blankets and sheets, and all the chocolate that his aunt kept up in the top cupboard. Plus we found five hundred dollars in cash and a bunch of silver jewelry.

We dumped it all into the truck, along with the gas can and the Weedwacker and the lawn mower and our bikes, and climbed in.

When we slammed the truck's doors, Miguel's neighbor Mrs. Olsen came out into her yard, holding a phone in her hand.

"Hey!" she shouted. "You can't drive!"

"Ignore her," Miguel said.

She started coming toward us, but Miguel turned the key and the Ford roared to life.

"Hey!" she called again, but she stopped coming after us—probably because she didn't want to get run over.

Miguel reversed the Ford and we started backing out. We went over the lawn and part of the curb, but the truck was so big, we hardly felt the bump. And then we were out on the street.

Miguel grinned at me, kind of crazy-like. "Where you want to go?"

I looked at Miguel, then down the street. With a shock, I realized we could probably go anywhere.

How far could you get in a truck with gas in the tank, and no one to care if you came home for dinner? With five hundred dollars, we could probably drive to the beaches of California, or down to Mexico, or way up north to Canada. It felt like we'd been cut free and could go anywhere. We could do anything we wanted.

And then I looked over at Miguel again, and I swear he was about to cry.

That's when it really hit me: No one cared if he came home ever again.

If his neighbor lady was on the ball and was actually calling the cops like it seemed, some social worker might eventually start hunting for him, but Miguel had no family. He was free, sure, but free like if you were tied to a giant helium balloon and were just going up and up and up until you ran out of air.

"My house," I said firmly. "We're going to my house. No one will ever find you there."

"You don't think?"

"We'll call you Manoj, or something. Say you're my cousin from Chicago. People can barely tell the difference between us, anyway."

We looked at each other, and then we both started to laugh. It was sad, and it was funny. Miguel put his foot on the gas and we peeled out, with his neighbor still watching from her lawn, her hand shading her eyes, holding her phone.

I watched her getting smaller and smaller in the truck's side mirror, still standing on the lawn, still trying to decide what to do about us, wondering if we were something she needed to worry about.

Nah, lady—we were going to do just fine.

CHAPTER 10

Miguel was a terrible driver: the truck was huge, and he was barely tall enough to see over the wheel and dashboard. He kept hitting the wipers instead of the turn signal and kept looking at the speedometer, so we almost went off the road a couple of times.

"Watch out!" I shouted when he grazed a mailbox.

"Quit complaining," he said. "This ain't *Gran Turismo*. Driving's harder than it looks."

"Just watch the road!"

Instead, Miguel ducked his head to look under the wheel and stomped on the wrong pedal. We braked suddenly. I slammed up against the dashboard and finally understood why my dad was always on me and Mom to wear our seat belts; my jaw hurt, and we hadn't even been going that fast.

"Oww!"

"Sorry," Miguel said. He gunned the engine, and we were off again.

We took side streets the whole way. I kept a lookout for police. At one point, there was a cop car, and we pulled over, and I was sure the cop was going to search us, because I had a creepy feeling the neighbor lady had already called us in. But the cop just kept going in a hurry and ignored us completely.

After we unloaded everything at the house, Miguel stood frowning at the truck. "We can't keep it here," he said.

"Why not?"

"Mrs. Olsen. She probably already reported it, and it leads right to us. We got to hide it somewhere."

I thought about it. "We could always put our bikes in the back and take it out to Milrow. If we leave the truck there, it just looks like your uncle could have driven it there. Might even be able to just keep it out there, and no one would care. They always got cars in their parking lot, from all the shifts."

"What if the cops find it and take it?"

"So they take it. It's not like you got a driver's license. If we keep driving it around, we're going to get caught for sure." When Miguel still hesitated, I said, "You definitely don't want ICE or the cops coming here, right?"

He nodded. "Yeah. I guess."

So we tossed our bikes back into the truck and drove out to the meatpacking plant.

We were going to go out the main road, but there was another police car, coming the other way, with its lights and sirens on. Miguel turned hard, and we headed down a side street, afraid we were caught for sure, but the cop just kept going.

"Where are all these cops coming from?" Miguel fumed.

"Dunno, but they don't seem to care about us."

We wound our way along smaller streets and eventually snuck back onto the highway. Miguel floored the gas. The big engine roared, and we blasted toward Milrow, with cornfields blurring beside us.

We found a parking place on the far side of the plant, over by Milrow Park, with a bunch of other workers' cars.

As we were getting out of the cab, I saw some of Miguel's aunt's jewelry on the floor and quickly scooped it up. "You almost forgot this."

Miguel cursed and we both checked over the rest of the cab, just to make sure. It turned out we'd missed a box of Count Chocula, and then Miguel found his glove and his bat and a bunch of his clothes that we'd shoved way down behind the seat.

"How are we going to get all this stuff back to your house?" Miguel asked.

"We aren't driving again," I said. "With all these cops around, our luck's definitely running out."

I had an idea. I started sorting through Miguel's clothes.

"What are you doing?"

I pulled on one of Miguel's sweatshirts. "We'll wear all the clothes," I said.

"Oh man, we'll boil."

"It's only for a couple miles," I said.

"This is how people get heatstroke, you know."

Miguel was right—the extra layers of clothing were killer hot, especially in the thick, humid air of Iowa summer. We managed to get everything on, and we stuffed the jewelry in our pockets.

"Who's taking the cereal?"

"I guess we leave it."

"And waste it?" I asked.

"It's really better with milk," Miguel said.

"My mom doesn't let me have this stuff," I said, and started digging out handfuls of the cereal and eating it. Miguel watched me like I was nuts. After a couple of mouthfuls, I knew why.

"It's really better with milk," Miguel said again.

"Gah." I spat out chocolate bits. "Thooo muth thugar."

Miguel just laughed at that. I was kind of glad; it was almost like he was coming back to normal.

"Come on, Einstein, let's get out of here." Miguel tossed me his baseball glove and balanced his bat across his handlebars, and we headed out.

Riding down the road, we looked like the dumbest dorks in the world with all our layers of clothing. Like Stay Puft Marshmallow Men on bikes. Almost immediately, we got passed by some high school kids who honked their horn and laughed and pointed.

"We look like bag ladies," Miguel groused.

"Well, you should've cleaned everything out when we had a chance. I'm sweating like a pig, and these aren't even my clothes," I said. My mouth still felt like a choco-sugar Sahara after eating all that cereal. "You owe me a root beer when we get back to town."

"You want *more* sugar?"

"I want *liquid* sugar. That's totally different."

Miguel started to answer, but broke off. The whine of a siren was rising in the distance, echoing over the cornfields.

"More cops?" I wondered. "Where are all these guys coming from?"

The siren was definitely coming our way, shrieking louder.

"Get off the road!" Miguel shouted.

We swerved into a ditch and dove flat beside our bikes. A second later, a cop car screamed past, lights and sirens blaring. We watched him whip by. Another followed, racing fast.

"That wasn't Delbe police," Miguel said, as we watched them disappear. "That's someone else."

Now that he mentioned it, I saw it, too. We'd been so focused on the lights and sirens that we hadn't noticed that they didn't have any town or state logos. Didn't say SHERIFF or POLICE or anything. They had stripes on the side, and lights and sirens, and they looked official, but they weren't from around here.

"Rent-a-cops?" Miguel guessed.

"ICE?" I asked.

"I don't think so. They sure aren't looking for me," Miguel said. "That one didn't even glance our way. And you were doing a crummy job of hiding."

It was weird. You just didn't see that many official vehicles zipping around Delbe, ever. And here we'd seen three or four, buzzing the roads like a herd of hornets. It was like they were looking for something—but they weren't stopping or slowing down, either. Just blasting back and forth.

As we got onto our bikes, another cop-like car shot by. We almost dove flat, but they really didn't seem to care about us at all.

"I guess we're safe," I said.

"Yeah. But let's get out of here while the getting's good."

We pedaled back toward town. Sweat dripped off our faces and soaked our layers of heavy clothes. All I could think of was how glad I was going to be to get into an air-conditioned house and drink an icy-cold root beer.

I guess it should have occurred to me that you don't get cop cars swarming like that if nothing important is going on. Sometimes, you just don't put two and two together until it's too late.

Or, in our case, it didn't happen until our baseball coach, Mr. Cocoran, stumbled out of the cornfields right in front of us.

CHAPTER 11

Mr. Cocoran raised his arm, and we slowed down. He was wearing his Milrow Meats work uniform, but it was ripped and spattered with brown stuff that smelled like cow manure, and there was a gash in his forehead dribbling blood down his face.

He looked terrible, and stunk even worse.

"Are you okay?" I asked.

Mr. Cocoran just stared at us, then looked back into the cornfields, where he'd left a trail of smashed and trampled corn. His eyes were wild and buggy, probably from the whack he'd taken to the forehead.

As we got closer, I saw that his uniform was covered with bits of corn silk and chunks of green leaves, like he'd been rolling and diving around in the corn all day.

On top of that, it looked like something had torn a couple of big chunks out of him, because his shoulder was all ripped and bloody.

"Mr. Cocoran?" I asked again. "Are you okay? Do you need a doctor?"

A fly buzzed around him and landed in the blood on his forehead. He didn't seem to mind. He opened his mouth like he wanted to say something. A weird sound gargled out. "Ghahaghahg."

He took a stumbling step toward me.

"Mr. Cocoran?"

"Gahaghg!" He made a clumsy lunge at me, opening his mouth and snapping his teeth. He lurched toward me again, his mouth open wide, like he was trying to bite me.

I rolled my bike backward. "Hey! Cut it out!"

"What's he doing?" Miguel asked.

"I have no idea!"

Mr. Cocoran kept stumbling after me, making clumsy grabs.

"Gahggh!" He caught my handlebars.

"Get off me, man!"

Instead, Mr. Cocoran grabbed my arm. He was really strong. He opened his mouth and tried to bite me again. I fell off my bike trying to twist away, but Mr. Cocoran held on tight. We landed in a pile, with Mr. Cocoran on top.

His teeth snapped again, going after my nose as we wrestled. I barely turned aside in time.

"GHAHAHGGHGHHH!"

His breath was hot and nasty, full of rot and disease. It took all my strength to keep his teeth away from my face.

"Get off!"

Drool ran from Cocoran's mouth in long streams. His tongue stuck out of his mouth, licking and lapping at me.

"Get off!"

He was too strong for me. Like Sammy, times ten. Miguel ran up and grabbed Mr. Cocoran, trying to pull him away, but Cocoran didn't budge.

"Get him off!" I shouted.

"I can't!" Miguel grunted. "He's too big!" Miguel jumped on the guy's back and tried to pry him away, but nothing did any good.

Mr. Cocoran's face pushed closer to mine, baring teeth. His rancid breath made me gag. I got my arm up against his neck, bracing against his throat, fighting to keep his nasty teeth from ripping into my skin. Miguel was still trying to roll him off or drag him away, but nothing was helping. My arm was weakening.

"I can't hold him, Miguel!" I shouted. "Get him off me already!"

"He's too strong!" Miguel yelled as he pulled on Mr. Cocoran's hair, yanking as hard as he could.

The man's face just got closer and closer.

"GaaahhhghHHEHGH!"

"Miguel…" I was using all my strength, and it wasn't enough.

Suddenly Mr. Cocoran let up.

For a second I thought he was letting me go. I thought he was going to say this was all some kind of a joke, and everything would go back to normal. Instead, he grabbed my arm…

And he *bit me*!

His teeth sank into my forearm. Even with all the clothes I had on, it hurt like crazy. I howled.

"*Get him off!*" I shouted to Miguel. "Get him off! Get him off, *gethimoffffffffff*!"

"I can't do anything!" Miguel shouted.

I was shaking my arm wildly, but Mr. Cocoran's teeth were sunk in deep. I couldn't get my arm loose. "Hit him! Just hit him! Use your baseball bat!"

So Miguel did.

Wham!

Right upside the head with his Louisville Slugger.

There was a wet *crunch*, and Mr. Cocoran's head snapped around. The guy fell off me and went still. I crawled out from under him, gasping, and hauled myself to my feet. We both stared down at Mr. Cocoran's flopped-over body.

"What the heck was that?" I couldn't get my breath back, and my body was shaking all over.

"You told me to hit him."

"I didn't say you should hit him in the *head*!"

"You're picky about *where* I hit him? He was tearing into you!" Miguel wiped the sweat off his face with a shaky arm.

"Oh man," I said, putting my hands to my forehead. "We are in so much trouble."

"Is he dead?" Miguel asked me, suddenly sounding worried.

Mr. Cocoran's head was dented, and his neck was all twisted around. "Well…" I said, "it doesn't look supergood."

I'll admit that I never really liked Mr. Cocoran, but seeing him lying there was sickening. One minute he'd been alive, and now he was just…gone. I rubbed my arm where he'd bitten me. I could barely touch it, it was so bruised.

"What are we supposed to do now?" Miguel wondered.

I had no idea. "I think when this happens in the movies, they hide the body."

"When this happens in movies? This isn't a movie!" Miguel was finally starting to freak out. "He wouldn't stop! I couldn't—" He broke off, looking shattered. "Oh man, this is bad."

The more we looked at Mr. Cocoran, the more I realized we were in serious trouble. You can't just go around hitting people with baseball bats. And it looked like Mr. Cocoran really was dead. One hit, and he'd gone down. Miguel really had an amazing swing.

"Does this mean we're murderers?" I asked.

It felt like the ground had gone missing below me. Like I was falling and falling and there wasn't any place to land. In one second, my whole life had changed, and there was no going back.

"We got to get out of here." Miguel grabbed my layers of shirts. "We just got to get out of here."

"No, wait. We need a plan," I said. "This wasn't our fault. It was self-defense, right?"

"Who cares! Let's figure out your superplan away from—"

Mr. Cocoran sat up.

Miguel and I yelped and jumped back.

"What the...?"

Mr. Cocoran's head was smashed in, and his neck was snapped over, but that wasn't stopping him. He dragged himself around, using his whole body to turn. His gaze fixed on us. Wide, hungry eyes rolled in their sockets.

"I thought you said he was dead," Miguel said, taking a farther step back.

"I thought he was!"

Mr. Cocoran hauled himself to his feet. He got one foot under him, then levered himself up until he could get his other foot set. He straightened and swayed in the hot sun.

Blood dripped from his mouth. More blood leaked from his smashed head, trickling down the side of his face.

He opened his mouth, showing ragged teeth and a gray tongue, slithery like a worm. He moaned and lurched toward us.

"Braaaaaains!"

CHAPTER 12

"Run!"

Miguel and I grabbed our bikes and tried to climb on, but you know how sometimes you jump on your bike too fast and you rack your nuts?

I totally did that.

It hurt so bad, I wanted to just curl up and puke, but with Mr. Cocoran coming after me, there was no time. I tried to get my feet on the pedals but I missed.

"Brrraaaaaaains!" Mr. Cocoran moaned.

Straddling my bike, I started hobbling down the road as fast as I could, while still trying to climb up onto my seat. I glanced back over my shoulder to see how close Mr. Cocoran was, and almost swerved off the road.

He was right behind me.

"Will you hurry up?" Miguel shouted as I almost crashed.

"I'm trying!"

My foot missed the pedal, and I scraped my shin. Mr. Cocoran took another swipe. I ducked and swerved, and his fingers whistled through my hair. Cocoran growled. He grabbed for my back tire. I swerved the other way, slipping and losing my pedals again.

"Quit fooling around!" Miguel shouted.

Finally—*finally*—my feet found the pedals.

I started riding like crazy.

I was going so fast, I shot past Miguel. I caught a glimpse of his surprised face as I went by, but I wasn't slowing down—no way, no how. Miguel raced to catch up, pedaling like we were in the Tour de France.

Behind us, Mr. Cocoran lost ground, but he was still reaching for us, and still moaning.

"Braaaaaaaiiiiinssssssssss!" It came out as a sad, hungry howl.

We didn't stop.

"What the heck was that all about?" Miguel shouted over the wind.

I had no idea what had just happened, but for sure I wasn't going back to figure it out. I just pedaled faster.

"I thought I killed him!" Miguel shouted.

"You did!"

And all of sudden, I realized that I actually liked that idea better. Killing a grown-up almost seemed normal in comparison to what had just happened.

This was worse.

Way worse.

If Miguel had beat Mr. Cocoran's head in with a baseball bat and the guy had died, that meant the world still worked the way we all thought it should. Sure, Miguel and I would probably get sent to a supermax prison or something, but still, it meant that the world hadn't just turned us upside down and shaken all the loose change out of our pockets.

If Mr. Cocoran had just gone ahead and died, the world still had rules.

But Mr. Cocoran hadn't died when Miguel had beaten his head in.

I guessed that was good in a way, because we weren't murderers now. But that also meant you could smash someone's head halfway in, and they could still stand up and try to bite your face again.

For sure, that wasn't right.

CHAPTER 13

"So, Rabi…" Miguel paused, as if he was trying to pick the right words. "What just happened back there?"

We were both sitting on the curb outside the Casey's convenience mart, sweating and exhausted, the sun beating down. I was yanking off layers and layers of clothing, trying to see my arm and desperate to cool off. My whole body was sticky and slimy. I wanted to go into the air-conditioning of the convenience mart, but I also wanted to be able to keep an eye on the road, just in case Mr. Cocoran came galloping down the centerline, yelling for our brains. I needed to be able to see him coming. I definitely needed to see him coming—

"Rabi?"

"I have no idea," I said as I dragged another layer over my head.

"'Cause if I didn't know any better, I'd say Mr. Cocoran was a zombie."

I didn't want to agree, but my own impressions were adding up the same way.

"He did say 'brains' when he was trying to bite me," I said.

I checked my arm. I'd been chomped so hard, a purple half-moon showed where his teeth had sunk in. I could actually see individual teeth impressions. I poked my finger into the dent an incisor had left.

At least I wasn't bleeding.

We both looked back toward where Mr. Cocoran was probably still wandering back and forth on the road, moaning for our brains. I kind of hoped a car would hit him.

And then I felt bad about it.

But then again, he really did try to bite my face off.

I decided I still hoped a car would run him over.

Had he really gotten up after Miguel whacked him? Had that all really happened? I looked at the three sweatshirts that I'd been wearing. Two of them were actually torn all the way through where Mr. Cocoran had ripped into them with his teeth. One less layer, and he would have gobbled a chunk of my arm, for sure.

"Zombies are impossible," Miguel said.

"I sure thought they were." I massaged my arm. "Then again, Mr. Cocoran did just stand up after getting walloped in the head. Check out what he did to my skin."

Miguel winced at the sight of the bruises. "Sooo...if he's a real zombie, that's kind of..."

"Bad?" I finished for him.

"Yeah. If it was for real, I mean."

"You know who we should ask about zombies?"

Miguel looked over, his eyes widening with the same thought.

"Joe!" we both said.

"He's the one who reads about this stuff all the time."

"Total zombie expert!"

I pulled on all of my ripped layers again, and we jumped on our bikes and rode over to Joe's house. When we got there, Joe was mowing his lawn, shirtless and sweating buckets in the sun.

"Hey, Joe," Miguel called. "You got to come with us. We got something you got to see."

"What's that?" Joe looked up, and started to laugh. "You guys look like a couple of dorks!"

I looked down at all my layers, then over at Miguel. We really did look like Stay Puft Marshmallow Men.

"Go ahead and laugh," I said. "It's armor."

"You're wearing, like, fifty shirts! In the summer!"

"Yeah, yeah, yeah. What do you know about zombies?" I asked.

"Zombies?"

"From all the stuff you read. What do you know about zombies?"

Joe rolled his eyes. "They eat brains for snacks. Now quit messing with me. I got to finish this before my dad gets home." He turned back to the lawn mower and gave a yank on the starter. The mower coughed but didn't start up.

"We think we saw one," I said.

"One what?"

"A zombie!" Miguel said.

Joe stopped trying to start the mower and gave us a disgusted look. "Come on."

"No, man, seriously. For real. Mr. Cocoran's a zombie."

"News flash."

"Seriously! Miguel beat his head in with a baseball bat, and he still tried to bite me."

That got Joe's attention.

"You hit Mr. Cocoran with a baseball bat?" He looked impressed. "I always wanted to do that."

"Well, Miguel did."

"No *way*."

Miguel grinned. Then he tried to look sorry. Then he just kind of shrugged. It was hard to decide what to think about it, except that I was glad Miguel had whacked Mr. Cocoran when he did. Because if he hadn't, I was pretty sure Mr. Cocoran would have chowed on my brains.

"Yeah. He really did it." I mimed Miguel's move. "*Bam!* Out of the park, snapped Cocoran's neck around, bent his head, everything."

"You're not kidding?" Joe was looking at us like we were crazy now. "You mean you *killed* him?"

I said, "That's the thing, though! *It didn't kill him.* It just bent him up a little. You got to see it. He isn't dead. Not a bit."

Joe looked like he couldn't decide if we were pulling his leg, or homicidal, or telling the truth.

Finally he said, "That's great, guys. Funny joke. Ha ha."

"It's not a joke!"

"Then why the heck would I go with you? I'd have to be stupid to go near a zombie. They're bad news."

"You chicken?" Miguel asked.

"I'm not chicken of something that doesn't exist! I got work to do! I'm in trouble enough on my own, without you guys getting me in more."

"Look, Joe," I said. "I swear there's a zombie running around in the cornfields. And you know more about zombies than anyone. So what are we supposed to do? How do you turn a zombie back into a person? Or kill it, or... You know... What are we supposed to do?"

"Well..." Joe shrugged. "Mostly they say you're supposed to shoot them in the head a couple of times. Double-tap to the head. That'll do it."

"We don't have guns."

"Bummer. And my dad keeps his locked up." Joe pulled his lip, considering. "I guess you could hit 'em like a baby seal until they stop flopping, then."

I could tell he wasn't taking us seriously.

"Fine," I said. "Don't believe us—you'll just never see it. We're going to catch a zombie and be heroes, and you're going to be the guy that could've seen the whole thing..."

"...except he decided to stay home and mow the lawn like a good little boy," Miguel finished.

Joe gave us a dirty look.

"Come on, Joe," I said. "You know you want to see this."

"I don't have time! I got to mow the lawn. My dad's going to whip me if I don't do it. Mom found out about my Amazon buy. I'm grounded again, and she took all my Transmetropolitans."

"This is better than a comic! It's a zombie! Don't you want to see a real live zombie?"

"Zombies aren't alive. They're undead."

"You see? That's why we need you! You know this stuff!"

Joe was looking from his house to the mower, and then to us. Wistful. Trying to decide. Wanting to do the crazy thing, but knowing it was wrong.

The cool thing about Joe is that when it comes to crazy...

"Lemme get my bike," Joe said.

...he can't resist.

"Get your bat, too!" I called out. "And don't forget some armor!"

CHAPTER 14

"Are you sure this is the right spot?" Joe asked.

We were riding slowly up and down the road, but there wasn't any sign of Mr. Cocoran.

"Pretty sure. It was just before the rise."

Joe looked at us with disgust. "Did you make this up?"

"No!" we both said at the same time. "He was right here."

We scanned the cornfields. I even got down on the road, looking for bloodstains. Maybe some piece of brain or something from his head. Nothing. It was like he'd never been there, and it had never happened.

"You jerks," Joe said. "My dad's going to whip my butt when I get home."

"But it happened!" I said.

"So where's Cocoran?"

Miguel was looking at the cornfields. "You think he went back into the corn?"

We all looked at the impenetrable jungle of cornstalks. No visibility. Thick and close. Hot.

"No way," I said. "No way am I going in there. That's definitely how people get killed in the movies. You go in, and you don't come out."

"I thought you said you wanted to show me the zombie," Joe goaded.

"Yeah," I said, "but I don't want to get bit again."

"You don't want to get bit *again*?" Joe looked at me with horror and started backing away.

"Just my arm, you sissy. It didn't break the skin. I was wearing all these shirts, so he didn't get through."

I rolled up my sleeve to show him, but Joe wouldn't come close.

"Come here, you baby," I said. "I'm not turning into a stupid zombie any more than you are."

"Sure," Joe muttered. "That's what everyone says in the movies, and the next thing you know, everyone's running and screaming, and their brains are popping out of their eyes, and there's blood all over the walls, and it's all because someone said they didn't get scratched."

Miguel and I exchanged glances. Joe sure watched some wacky movies.

"Well, I didn't get scratched, and you can take a look. And anyway, this isn't a movie. This is real life."

Joe snickered at that. "So where's your real-life zombie?"

The cornfields were probably where Cocoran had gone. But boy, I sure didn't want to go in there. If Cocoran jumped on us from behind or something…

On the other hand, I really, *really* didn't want Joe telling everyone that we were a couple of liars for bringing him out here for nothing.

"Okay," I said. "We'll go in. But we're taking our bats."

"Which side of the road?"

"He came from that side when we ran into him. Maybe he went back the way he came."

"This is nuts," Miguel said. "We're not going to find him. There's miles and miles of corn out here. It's like trying to find a needle in a haystack."

"A zombie in a cornfield," Joe said.

"Cornfield zombies," I said.

"Corn-fed zombies," Miguel said.

"Zombies in the corn," Joe said.

We all started to laugh. "That would make a pretty good video game," I said. "*Zombies in the Corn*."

"*Left 4 Dead* already did it."

"Not with corn."

"Because it would be corny," Joe said.

"Ha ha." I got my bat. "You guys ready?"

But Joe and Miguel didn't move.

"What now?" I asked.

"Well...who's going in first?" Miguel asked.

"Not me," Joe said. "I'm just along for the ride."

"I thought you didn't believe us," I said.

"I thought you said there was a zombie in the corn."

Standoff.

"Okay, I'll go first," I said finally.

I didn't like it, but it made for good strategy. "You guys are stronger hitters than me, anyway. I'll go in first and be the bait. When I smoke out the zombie, you guys whack him before he chews my brains out."

But that didn't mean I was going in unprepared.

"Gimme your shirts," I said. "All of them. If I'm going first, I'm taking all the armor."

Miguel and Joe stripped off their extra layers, and I put them on. Lots and lots and lots of layers. Stay-Puft-Marshmallow-Michelin-Man zombie bait. But at least there was no way Cocoran's teeth were going to bite through that much fabric. At least I hoped.

I grabbed my bat. "If Cocoran jumps me, you guys better hit the bejesus out of him. I don't know how much biting these shirts can take."

"Right," Joe said. "Hit the bejesus out of him."

"Hit him in the head," Miguel advised. "That got his attention the last time."

"Yup. The head. No problem."

You could tell Joe still didn't believe us. I wondered if I was crazy to be trusting my life to someone as goofy as Joe. He couldn't even take things seriously when it was life or death.

"Pay attention, Joe," I said. "If Cocoran tries to grab me, you got to get him off me fast. Hit him in the head, like Miguel says."

"And try not to hit Rabi," Miguel added.

"What's that supposed to mean?" Joe asked.

Miguel shrugged. "Sometimes, you swing wild."

"I do not."

"You miss more than you hit."

"I think I can hit a guy's head," Joe groused. "It's a heck of a lot bigger than a baseball."

We headed into the corn.

CHAPTER 15

Green corn whipped our faces as we shoved through. The air trapped between the dense rows was hot and still and humid, like a jungle. It wasn't exactly a stealth operation; stalks crackled and snapped, announcing our every step.

We all had our baseball bats up and ready to swing, but Mr. Cocoran didn't show.

I stopped in the middle of the corn. A second later, Miguel and Joe forced their way through to where I was. Corn silk and green leafy bits stuck to their flushed necks and faces.

"We're doing this wrong," I said. "Let's go back to the road."

"Why?"

"Because if Cocoran went in, we don't want to search for him, we want to *track* him."

That made sense to everyone, so we returned to the open road and started walking up and down the pavement's edge.

"Look for broken plants. Maybe some blood. He wasn't walking too good, so he probably smashed into some things."

After a while, Joe called, "Got it!"

He was farther up the road than I expected, but he was standing beside some bashed-down cornstalks. And on the road, there were a couple of big bloodstains, turned sticky on the pavement, with flies buzzing in the goo.

"Now do you believe us?" I asked.

He shrugged. "Could have been a raccoon for all I know."

"A raccoon that knocks down corn?" I rolled my eyes. "Let's go."

We started into the corn again, bats up. It wasn't a great trail, but it was enough. The corn was so dense that you couldn't go through the thick walls of it without breaking at least some stalks. The biggest problem with tracking Mr. Cocoran was that he also wasn't supergood at going in a straight line. He went around in circles, he doubled back. He zigged and zagged and staggered.

"Haven't we seen this spot before?" Miguel asked as we stumbled into a trampled clearing.

"I can't tell," Joe said, waving at a cloud of flies that had started swarming us. "This is like tracking a drunk cow."

"Let's try this way," I suggested, choosing a broken path through the corn that I didn't think we'd followed already. "He's got to be out here somewhere."

"You sure this is for real?" Joe asked.

"Of course it's real," Miguel said. Then he grinned at me. "Lead on, zombie bait."

"Quit saying that," I said.

Miguel's smile widened. "Don't worry, zombie snack, I got your back."

And that was enough to get Joe going. He started trying to make up limericks about zombies and snacks.

"Rabi went into the corn,
Playing bait on zombie morn.
When it attacked,
Rabi's brain was a snack,
And he wished he'd never been born."

"Real cute, Joe."

"I was trying to use *Rabindranath*, but that takes up way too many syllables." He launched into another one:

"There once was a zombie named Splatter,
Who ate Rabi's brains on a platter...."

I gave Joe a dirty look. "Just remember the plan. I'm only on point so you can get a clear whack at him while he goes after me. You better hit the heck out of him."

"Swing? Fling? Whack? Smack?"

"Don't worry, buddy," Miguel said. "We'll lay your zombie flat."

Joe's eyes lit up. "That's a good one."

Miguel laughed and we kept going, while Joe worked on his poetry. You had to hand it to him, even with all the heat, Joe didn't tire out. Just kept rhyming. Flat. Splat. Flood. Blood. Brains. Plantains. Guts. Nuts. He wasn't good, but he was relentless.

Flies buzzed around us. The corn rustled. I couldn't see more than a foot ahead. "What's that smell?" I asked finally, holding up my hand and interrupting Joe.

Miguel sniffed. "Smells like cow sewage. From the feedlots."

"That's nasty," Joe said.

"How come it's so strong?" I wondered.

We kept hacking through the corn, and then suddenly the stalks parted and we had our answer. We were standing on the edge of a giant pool of cow manure.

A lagoon.

A sea.

An ocean of poop.

On the far side, way off in the distance, there were a bunch of fenced corrals, stuffed to the brim with hundreds and hundreds of cows, all mooing and bumping into one another and waiting to get pushed into the Milrow Meats beef-processing facility, which was even farther beyond.

In all of our twistings and turnings, I hadn't realized that we'd ended up walking so close to Milrow.

Flies swarmed everywhere, thick clouds of them. The air stank.

"Yech. Now what?" Miguel asked.

"You think Cocoran fell into the poop?" Joe asked, as we all tried to keep from gagging.

"Who knows what a zombie does?" I said. "You're supposed to be the expert."

"He'd drown," Miguel said.

"Does a zombie even breathe?" I asked.

A second later, we had our answer.

"Oh. My. *God.*" Joe's eyes bugged out of his head.

All our eyes bugged out of our heads.

On the far side of the lagoon, something was crawling out of the manure lake.

It was a person, completely covered in liquid cow goo.

It stood up.

"Is that Mr. Cocoran?" Joe asked.

I elbowed him in the ribs. "I *told* you he was a zombie! No real live person would swim in that!"

"That's the most disgusting thing I've ever seen."

Except it wasn't, because right after that, the zombie flopped over the feedlot fence and attacked the cows, and that was even more disgusting than just being a zombie covered head to toe with cow manure.

The cows backed away from the zombie, but it kept going after them, herding them as they ran back and forth, trying to escape.

The zombie wasn't very good at chasing, because it was slow, but it didn't stop, either. Finally the zombie caught a cow by the leg and bit in. The cow went bonkers, mooing and galloping around and dragging the zombie with it. The zombie bounced up and down, and manure spattered everywhere as the cow shook it, but the zombie didn't let go. It got a better hold on the cow, climbed onto its back, and started tearing in.

"Am I really seeing this?" Joe asked.

"Well, I am," Miguel answered.

The cow kept banging around, but the zombie hung on like a tick. It started chewing into the cow's head.

Deeper and deeper. Finally the cow just fell over, and the zombie started to chow down.

Miguel and Joe and I watched the zombie snarf cow brain.

Miguel whistled. "That could have been you, Rabi."

That's when Mr. Cocoran burst out of the corn.

CHAPTER 16

"Braaaaaiiiiiiiiiiins!"

"Aaaaahhhhggh! Run away!"

Of course, we immediately forgot my whole zombie-fighting plan and bolted in three completely different directions.

Unfortunately, Mr. Cocoran decided I was the one to chase. I don't know if it was because he remembered me from our last run-in on the highway, or if he had something against me from telling him how to run his baseball team, but he ignored Miguel and Joe and zeroed right in on me.

I plowed through the corn, shoving stalks aside. I couldn't run nearly fast enough because the corn was so dense. I thrashed and smashed and kicked and hacked my way through, gasping for air, and Cocoran came right behind. I started getting a stitch in my side. I felt dizzy from the heat and all the clothes I was wearing.

Cocoran groaned hungrily. He was getting closer.

There was no way I was going to make it back to the highway at this rate. I needed help.

"Where are you guys?" I shouted.

I thought I heard someone shouting off in the distance, but I couldn't slow down to listen. The corn whipped my face and slashed my skin.

"I'm over here!" I shouted. "Help me, will you!"

Behind me, Mr. Cocoran moaned. "Braaiinnss!"

I wasn't going to make it to the road. I was just too slow, fighting through the corn. It was time to change strategies. When I hit a slightly trampled spot in the corn, I turned and brought up my Louisville Slugger. I'd just have to fight him.

Mr. Cocoran came right at me.

Set your stance.

Keep your eye on the ball.

Cocoran's head was coming in high. Way out of the strike zone. It would have been a ball for sure if we'd been in a game. His head was all mashed up, and one of his eyes was looking off in a whopper-jawed direction. It made me remember something from American History—

George Washington or someone saying you were supposed to wait till you saw the whites of their eyes before attacking.

Mr. Cocoran's eyes were almost all white. Creepy, milky white.

He came in fast.

"BrraaAAAAIIIIINNNNSSsssss!"

Keep your eye on the ball and—

I swung as hard as I could.

Bam!

Total connection. Mr. Cocoran's head snapped sidewise. It was probably the best baseball hit I'd ever had. Got him right with the fat part of the bat. I felt a rush of triumph as he piled past me.

But then Cocoran turned and started in on me again.

My skin crawled. I'd hit him a good one and knocked him off course, but here he was, coming right back. I hadn't slowed him down at all.

"BRAii—"

I hit him again. Bounced the bat off his skull and ducked under his flailing arms to get behind him. He didn't seem to mind, though. Just came back at me again. Zombies were tough!

I heard Miguel and Joe calling for me.

"I'm over here!" I shouted. "Where are you?"

"*Rabi?*"

"Hurry up!"

Mr. Cocoran attacked again. It was just like in real life—Mr. Cocoran wasn't supersmart, but he sure was stubborn. My dad always said that having a mule-headed personality only got you so far, but I was starting to think it was going to be enough for Mr. Cocoran to get a seat at the all-you-can-eat Rabi brain buffet.

My arms were getting tired, and I was gasping for air. Running and swinging and dodging zombies took a lot more energy than just playing baseball.

"BRAAAAIIIIIINNNNSSSSS!"

I swung again, but this time, Mr. Cocoran got his hands up. Bone crunched, and one of his arms snapped. The other hand grabbed my bat. In a blink, he tore it from my grasp.

Uh-oh.

Mr. Cocoran smiled—or whatever was left of Mr. Cocoran, anyway. His tongue stuck out, gray and wormy, and you could tell he was looking forward to chewing me to pieces. I took a step back.

Just then, Joe and Miguel came thrashing through the corn. Two big guys, coming fast and furious.

Wham!

Miguel laid his bat into the back of the zombie's head. *Bam!*

Joe slammed the zombie's hand that held my bat. The zombie went down. He tried to get up again, but this time, I wasn't going to let that happen.

"Get his knees!" I shouted. "You can't kill him by hitting his head! I already tried! Get his knees so he can't chase us!"

Wham!

Bam!

Slam!

Whack!

Crack!

Crunch!

Zombie legs shattered. Arms got obliterated.

The monster snapped his battered teeth at us. Without working arms or legs, all he could do was lie there, staring up at us with creepy, milky zombie eyes, tongue licking the air.

"Braaaaaiiiiiinnnnsss," the thing whispered.

He didn't seem to notice that his arms and legs weren't working anymore. He sniffed the air.

"Braaaiiiins."

He started trying to inchworm his way toward us.

"Yo, dude," Joe said. "That ain't right."

"Now do you believe us?" I asked.

"Oh yeah. That's a zombie, all right. One hundred percent USDA pure homegrown American zombie, for sure."

Mr. Cocoran's zombie teeth kept snapping. We realized that we all had blood on us.

"Um. Joe?" I asked.

"Yeah?"

"Do you know if we can get zombified by zombie blood?"

Joe thought about it. "I don't know. All the comic books say you got to get bitten."

"Yeah, but this is a real zombie. We aren't in a comic book."

Joe puzzled on that some more. "Beats me. I know doctors and nurses don't like getting blood on them in the hospital."

The spatters were all over us. My skin crawled. Mr. Cocoran moaned again.

"Brains brains brainssss."

He sounded like a loop in a techno mix.

"We got to get washed up," I said.

"What do we do about Mr. Cocoran?" Miguel asked.

Joe frowned. "My grandma and grandpa, they sometimes put a farm dog down when it gets too old. Same for cows and horses."

"So...what? We just got to keep beating on him until he stops moving?"

We all looked down at the zombie monster.

"I'm not doing it," Miguel said.

I couldn't help agreeing, and Joe looked sick at the thought, too. Even if he was a zombie, no one wanted to do the job. It was one thing to snap a zombie's arms and legs and make sure it couldn't bite you, but it was another thing to keep pounding on it until it was dead.

Mr. Cocoran bared his teeth at us again.

"Let's just leave him," I said, finally.

"Are you serious?"

"It's not like he's going anywhere," I said. "We'll go find the police and bring them back. They can figure out what to do with him."

"We going to tell them that we hit Mr. Cocoran until we broke his arms and legs, too?" Miguel asked. "And his head? You know that'll get me deported, for sure."

Joe looked surprised. "Who the heck's going to deport you?"

In all the excitement, we'd forgotten to tell Joe everything else that was going on.

"Miguel's uncle and aunt just got picked up by ICE," I explained.

"When did that happen?"

"Today."

"Why'd ICE pick up your aunt and uncle?"

I was about to answer that we didn't know, but my eyes were drawn to Mr. Cocoran. He was still wearing his torn-up Milrow Meats uniform. He smiled and stuck out his gray zombie tongue at us.

"Brains," he hissed. *"Brainsssss."*

Milrow Meats…Zombies…Miguel's uncle talking about bad things he'd seen…

Puzzle pieces started to click into place. "Maybe they saw something they weren't supposed to," I said.

"Maybe they were making trouble," Miguel added, nodding.

"Like your dad," I said. "Like when he complained about Milrow speeding up the line and said that it wasn't safe for workers."

It was making sense, all of a sudden. Sammy Riggoni hadn't been the guy who'd gotten Miguel's aunt and uncle taken away; it had been Sammy's dad. The big cheese at Milrow, who had stood in front of the TV cameras and said that the weird smells were totally normal. But what if a bunch of his workers knew different? And what if they were thinking about talking? The answer would be simple. Just get them deported, so there wouldn't be anyone to complain. And Sammy had just found out about it. That's why he'd been gloating.

"I bet ICE took a bunch of people today," I said. "Not just your aunt and uncle."

Joe was focused on something different, though. "So you don't have *any* family anymore?" he asked Miguel.

"Yeah," Miguel said. "That's about the size of it."

"You need someplace to live—" Joe broke off. "I mean, my dad's a pain in the neck, but I got a top bunk in my room. I can clean it off. You can totally live with us."

"Nah."

"Seriously, man. I can move all my comics. Put them in the shed or something. I need to get them out anyway. There's room. I can *make* room."

"I don't think it works like that," Miguel said. "I think they put kids like me in foster homes."

"Forget that!" Joe said. "You didn't ask to be an orphan! You're staying with us."

"He's staying with me for a little while," I said.

"Yeah," Miguel said. "We're going to tell Social Services that I'm his cousin Manoj."

Joe laughed at that. "You'd better start learning how to dance like they do in those Bollywood movies that Rabi's got, or they'll never believe it."

"We've got a couple of weeks until Rabi's mom comes back. I'll figure something out."

Joe snorted. "Get ready to bust a move, Manoj."

Just then, Mr. Cocoran snapped his teeth. He'd been inching over to us. If he'd had any arms left, he'd have snagged Joe for sure.

We all skipped back, shouting and lifting up our baseball bats, ready to beat him down if he got back up. But of course he didn't; he just lay there like a big floppy fish, smiling with his nasty, hungry mouth and groaning.

"*Braaaaiiiiiinssssssssssssss.*"

"Let's go get the police," I said. "We can leave Miguel out of it. But we'd better tell some grown-ups before this gets out of hand. We're in way over our heads."

✳ ✳ ✳

"Fighting zombies in real life is totally different than in *Left 4 Dead*," Joe said.

We were headed back toward the highway, feeling

kind of triumphant about winning a fight with a zombie.

"How's it different?" Miguel asked.

"In the game, you got to worry about the zombies swarming, and they're superfast. You got to keep blasting away, to get them all. It's like a zombie mob—"

I stopped short and Joe and Miguel slammed into my back.

"What the—"

"Would you keep walking?" Miguel said.

"There's another zombie," I said.

In the excitement of being chased by Mr. Cocoran, we'd completely forgotten it.

Joe groaned. "The poop zombie."

"Yeah. The one that was chewing on the cow."

"You think it made the cow into a zombie?" Joe asked.

"Can cows get zombied?" Miguel asked.

"I think they're too dumb to be zombies," Joe said. Then he shrugged. "On the other hand, up until twenty minutes ago, I didn't think people could get zombied, either."

"There was another zombie," I said. "Mr. Cocoran wasn't the only one. That means other people could be catching it."

"How do you think Mr. Cocoran got it?" Miguel asked.

"He had on his Milrow uniform," Joe said. "I bet he caught it working there."

Miguel punched him in the shoulder. "My aunt and uncle worked there, too. And they aren't zombies."

"Not the last time you saw them."

Miguel gave him a dirty look. "I think someone at ICE would have noticed if they showed up to check immigration papers and ended up fighting zombies. If Mr. Cocoran got turned into a zombie at Milrow, then he had to be doing something different than my family. They worked on the production line."

"You guys," I broke in, "it doesn't matter where it started! What matters is that we've seen two zombies in the space of twenty minutes. Think about it."

Joe and Miguel exchanged glances. "Whoa," Joe said.

"*Dios mío*," Miguel said. "There could be more."

"A lot more," I said.

"There could be millions! Total zombie apocalypse!" Joe said, and then he looked thoughtful. "That would be pretty cool, actually. I mean, if they didn't all want to chew our brains out."

Trust Joe to find the bright side of the zombie apocalypse.

"I doubt it will be millions," I said. "We only got about two thousand people in the whole town."

The cornfields opened ahead of us. "Two thousand might not be millions," Miguel said, as we picked up our bikes, "but if we're not careful, we could still be up to our armpits in zombies."

CHAPTER 17

At my house, we all took showers to get the blood off. Just in case it was infectious, we dumped a bunch of iodine and hydrogen peroxide all over ourselves, too. I wasn't sure if it would do any good, but I figured it was better than nothing.

After that, Joe and I rode over to the police station.

The guy at the front desk gave us a bored look.

"Yeah?"

"We want to report a zombie uprising," Joe said, before I could stop him.

The police guy smirked. "You want to report a vampire hive, too?"

"We're serious—"

I cut Joe off before he could dig a deeper hole. "We

saw a guy out in the cornfields. He looked like he needed help. He's all beat-up."

The police guy's eyebrows went up. "You're reporting an assault?"

Was it an assault if you broke the arms and legs of a *zombie*?

I said, "I don't know how he got like he was, but he looked pretty bad."

"All bloody!" Joe added.

Right then, we lost the police guy again. "Yeah? And did he keep asking for brains?"

"Well," Joe said, "he wasn't really asking, so much as moaning."

The policeman leaned over his desk. "You think pranks like this are hilarious, don't you? Maybe you've got some friends out there, laughing because they dared you to come in here and waste my time..."

His eyes narrowed. "I've got real work to do here, and we've got real crimes to deal with." He made a dismissive gesture. "Beat it."

I tried again. "Really, sir. It's not a joke. The man, he's named Mr. Cocoran and he was our Little League coach. And he's out in the cornfields outside of town, and he doesn't look right. We aren't lying, and it isn't a joke. My friend likes comic books and he likes to tell stories, but

that's not his fault. He's just that way. But Mr. Cocoran . . .
We think he's in real trouble. Couldn't you just drive out
and check on him?"

The man looked at me. "We're kind of busy right now."

"Please. We'll go with you. If we're lying, you can
throw us in jail."

He sort of smiled at that.

"That's not quite how it works." He looked up at the
clock. "All right. I'll call an officer. You can show him."

CHAPTER 18

I wasn't convinced that Officer Boone really was an officer. Maybe a trainee or something. Or maybe he was, like, a high school kid they'd dressed up in a police uniform. Sort of like they have those dummies out in California that sit in squad cars by the side of the highway and look like they're shooting you with a radar gun, but actually they're just sitting there being dummies—because you know they're stuffed, right?

Officer Boone might have had a uniform, but his face looked like a baby's. Pale-blond hair, superpale pink skin, blue eyes. He should have been wearing diapers.

Joe had the same thought. He took one look at Officer Boone and whispered that we had Officer Baby Face with us. He looked so young, I was surprised they gave him keys to drive a car. Miguel looked older than this guy. I mean, Miguel was actually starting to grow a mustache. This guy wasn't going to be shaving until he was eighty.

I hoped his gun was real, at least.

Baby Face Boone drove us out into the increasing dusk, as we told him where to go. Then we got out and started walking, following our trail back through the corn.

"You can get your gun out now," I said.

Boone looked at me like I was an idiot. "How about we just find this Mr. . . . Cocoran, okay, kid?"

I wanted to say, "Sure, kid." But I didn't.

Officer Baby Face also didn't take his gun out. I wanted to say, *Buddy, when a zombie comes to rip your brains out, you're going to wish you had your gun.* But I didn't. I just headed out into the corn, feeling naked because I didn't have enough layers of clothing, and wishing I had my bat.

Baby Face Boone, the slowest draw in Iowa.

Weee.

Without any kind of decent backup, Joe and I took it slow, listening to the corn and hoping we weren't about to be ambushed by any other zombies.

We finally got to the spot where we'd fought Mr.

Cocoran. I could tell it was the right spot, because everything was trampled, but...

We stopped short.

"What the—?" Joe muttered.

The corn was stomped down, but that was all.

"It was right here," I said.

Boone swung a big old flashlight around, its beam sending hungry shadows swirling. Every time he did it, my skin crawled, but there wasn't any Mr. Cocoran, and there wasn't any zombie. There wasn't even any blood. Just missing corn and some dug-up dirt.

"It was right here!" I said.

"It?" Officer Boone asked.

"I mean Mr. Cocoran," I said.

"You sure?" he asked. "I don't see anything."

"There's no blood," Joe said. He circled around. "Check it out. Some of the corn's missing. Looks like it was dug up."

"You want to report a theft of corn now?" Boone asked.

Joe was right, though. The area was totally cleared out, and the dirt was turned over and scuffed. There weren't any of our footprints in it, and no blood, either. We'd had a whole zombie battle, and now the evidence was gone, like aliens had landed and scooped it up and taken it all away.

"You think maybe he crawled out of here?" Joe wondered.

"He couldn't have."

"Why not?" Officer Boone asked.

We exchanged glances. "Uhh…"

Because we broke every bone in his arms and legs so all he could do was squirm around like an inchworm and say "brains" over and over again.

But we couldn't admit that.

"Just because."

Officer Boone was starting to get angry. "Is this a prank?" he asked. "Is this your idea of a funny joke?"

It didn't matter how many times we said *No, sir, we're not joking, sir, he was here, sir* as we crawled around on the ground, trying to find evidence, Officer Boone just got more and more annoyed.

Finally he said, "All right, boys. You've wasted enough of my time." He stomped off to his car.

No way were me and Joe going to stick around in dark cornfields without the guy with the gun. Even if he was Baby Face. We ran after him.

Of course when we got back into the car, it got worse, because Boone got on the radio and reported that he hadn't seen anything, zombie or otherwise—and then as soon as he did that, the dispatcher squawked and asked if "those kids" were still with him.

"Yeah, I still got 'em," he said into his radio.

"Bring them in. Rabi..." The dispatcher hesitated. "Rabidmath Chatterjee is wanted for questioning."

Uh-oh. That couldn't be good.

Miguel. It had to be. They wanted Miguel and a certain missing red F-250 pickup truck, for sure.

I hit the handle on the door and tried to jump out of the car, but Boone beat me to it. He hit a button and the doors locked and I just slammed up against glass.

He grinned at me in the rearview mirror. "Nice try, kid."

He started up the car and put it in gear. I was going to jail for sure. I wondered if my mom could bring me mango pickle and rice, or if I'd have to eat jail food all the time. And then I wondered if jail food was worse than Delbe Middle School food.

"Are we under arrest?" I asked.

Baby Face Boone didn't answer.

CHAPTER 19

If you ever get picked up by the cops, just deny everything and ask for a lawyer.

I learned that from *Law & Order*. So when they got me into a room with a bald guy with glasses and a full beard going white, who looked a little like Santa Claus, I kept mum.

"I want a lawyer," I said.

Santa Claus said, "That's not the way it works, kid. You're not charged with anything. We just need to ask you some questions. We're looking for a friend of yours. A Miguel Castillo."

"Don't know him. Don't know where he is."

"No?" the detective looked surprised. "His neighbor said you two drove away in Mr...." the detective, whose name was Pearson, looked at his papers. "Mr. Castillo's—his uncle's—truck. A maroon Ford F-250 extended cab. Just this afternoon."

"So?" I said.

I felt bad about stonewalling—because my mom would have died if she knew I'd talked like that to a grown-up—but I'd seen enough cop shows to know that you can't back down.

"So you saw him this afternoon?" the detective asked. "At his house? When you pulled..." He looked at his notes again. "Three suitcases, eight pillowcases, two armloads of sheets and blankets, four boxes of cereal, a lawn mower, two bikes, a Weedwacker, and a large plastic—possibly ten-gallon—jug of gasoline, into said F-250 extended cab and fled the scene?"

Uh.

"I want a lawyer," I said.

Pearson rolled his eyes and leaned forward. "Let me tell you how this works, kid. Either you answer my questions—and you stop talking about lawyers and whatever you learned from watching *Castle*, or *Law & Order*, or whatever cop show that you think told you something about how to 'beat the man'—or you keep on making my life difficult, and I put you into the holding cells with all the drunks and the bikers who came through town yesterday. And maybe, if I remember, you see a lawyer tomorrow. Or the next day. So you either help me out and quit trying to be a hard case, or you keep making my life crummy on a nice summer Wednesday night."

He looked over his glasses at me. "Think about it. Keep asking for that lawyer. I'm begging you. See how it goes for you."

"But I didn't do anything!" I protested.

"Driving without a license is a serious crime."

"I wasn't the one who was driving!"

"So Miguel was driving?"

Dang. I wasn't so good at the criminal thing after all. You aren't supposed to rat out your buddies. I tried to figure a way out. "Uhhhh…"

"Quit dragging this out"—he checked the report in front of him—"Rabidmath."

"That's not how you say my name."

"Just tell us where he is."

What was I supposed to do? I couldn't give up Miguel. No way. If they got hold of him, there was no telling what they'd do—

And then, inspiration.

"He's gone to Mexico," I said.

The detective looked at me like I'd just told him that Miguel had decided to become a violin-playing penguin.

I repeated myself. "He's gone to Mexico. He's going to find his family."

"He's thirteen years old!"

"He's got five hundred dollars and a truck. And it's an automatic."

The detective glared at me. Then he got up and went to the door, and called out. "Hey! Bernie! See if we've got any traffic stops out toward I-80, or heading south to Kansas."

He came back. "We'll see if you're telling the truth."

"He's taking the back roads," I said. "You'll never catch him."

The detective looked at me, then he sighed. "You might be right about that, kid." He paused. "So, where's your parents?"

"My mom's in India, and my dad's in North Dakota on an oil derrick. He's out of cell phone reach."

"More stories?"

"No! My mom really is in India. Her sister's in the hospital. I was supposed to be staying with Miguel, but then ICE went and grabbed his aunt and uncle." I looked at him. "Can I stay at your place until my mom gets back?"

He looked disgusted. "Your mother ought to be arrested for neglect." He tapped his pen on the table, thinking. *Tat-tat-tat.* "We'll have to put you into some kind of temporary housing until we can find a responsible adult," he decided.

Responsible adult. That was kind of a funny one. Responsible adult. I wondered where they were, exactly. My dad was working; my mom was gone. Miguel's family were all taken, and they'd been about the most responsible people I'd ever met. His family had always been on Miguel to study and get good grades and all that. And they worked like crazy, doing shifts at the plant and then lawn care on the weekends and housecleaning, too. They'd been awesome, but ICE had scooped them up. Joe's parents? Joe's dad was a mean old drunk about half the time, and the rest of the time he was working, and Joe's mom only did things like shop and sit around and watch TV.

And now something really bad was happening, and no one was paying any attention at all.

Responsible adults.

The zombie apocalypse was coming, and the people who were supposed to do something about it were busy calling around looking for a social worker and filing paperwork. They were trying to track down a kid who didn't *want* them to find him because their version of help was to stick him with some family that wasn't his.

I knew if I told this cop about the zombie apocalypse, he'd say I was making up wing-ding stories, and then he'd come down on me even harder than he already was.

Responsible adults.

Let's face it. They say they're responsible, but half the time, they just make things worse, and the other half of the time, they're so clueless, they might as well be out of the picture.

I guessed that my dad might have believed me, if he'd actually been here. But since he wasn't, it looked like we were on our own if we were going to stop the zombie apocalypse.

And that meant I had to find some way to bust out of jail.

CHAPTER 20

Detective Pearson didn't put me in a holding cell. He had me sit on a chair in the office where the detectives worked, while he typed stuff into his computer and called around to figure out where he could dump me with a "responsible adult."

I sat there picking at the laces on my sneakers and trying to figure out if I could just make a run for it.

"I'm here for Rabindranath Chatterjee-Jones."

Someone pronouncing my name correctly? That caught my attention.

A tall guy wearing a suit and tie and carrying a brief-case was standing behind the counter. He caught sight of me, peeking out of the detectives' office. He had small rectangular glasses that looked city-slick, and he was completely bald. He sort of reminded me of someone, but I couldn't quite place him...

"Rabindranath?" the suit guy asked. "Rabi?"

How did he know me?

Detective Pearson was moving to get between us.

"What's your business?" the desk sergeant and Pearson said at the same time.

The bald suit guy grinned, and suddenly it hit me—the guy looked almost exactly like Spider Jerusalem. Minus the tattoos and cigarettes, sure, and all dressed up, too. But with that crazy smile, all the guy needed was a takeout carton of caribou eyeballs, and he could have been the spitting image.

Bald suit guy said, "My business is with my client Rabindranath Chatterjee-Jones, whom you have been holding without charge or bail."

"Wait just a second—" Pearson started, but the guy mowed him down.

"You have held him without charge or bail, and..." He peered around Pearson's Santa Claus body to see me. "Did you ask for a lawyer, Rabi?"

I nodded vigorously. Pearson glared at me. The suit guy tore into him, his voice getting louder.

"You have held my client without charge or bail, and you have prevented my client from retaining counsel. At this point, I could probably bring you up in both criminal and civil court for kidnapping, dereliction of duty, civil rights violations—"

"Who the heck are you?" Pearson demanded.

Spider Jerusalem, I thought. *Kicking the butt that deserves it.*

"Lawrence Maximillian, of Maximillian, Young, and Trevaine." He bared his teeth. "We specialize in police-brutality cases."

Pearson started to protest. "We were looking for a responsible adult!"

"For more than four hours? Did you let my client call me?"

"He didn't ask for you!"

"He asked for a lawyer. Did you even provide a public defender? Read him his rights? *Anything?*"

I didn't know who this guy was, but he was brilliant. Every time Pearson tried to say something, the suit dude just hammered back.

Whenever I get in an argument, I never have a comeback when I really want it. I think of responses a week later, and then I never get to use them. This lawyer was amazing.

Pearson said, "Protective custody."

Lawyer guy said, "Civil rights."

Pearson said, "Couldn't locate."

Lawyer guy said, "No charge."

Bam, bam, bam. Out of the park, every time.

And then the lawyer guy just said, "Come on, Rabi, we're leaving."

I looked to the cops, and then at the lawyer.

"Hold it right there," Pearson said.

Lawrence Maximillian said, "Don't even stop, Rabi."

"You're interfering with an investigation."

"You're interfering with my client's freedom. Charge him now, in my presence. Please. Make my day. We'll have Judge Fenton on the phone, and we'll start the paperwork for our lawsuits and your procedural errors, at the same time." The lawyer stared Pearson down. "I eat police departments like yours for lunch. When I'm done with you, you'll be selling Skittles and Gatorade at a Casey's convenience mart, and the town of Delbe will be bankrupt."

He took my arm. "Come on, Rabi. They're done talking to you."

"Are you sure?" I asked.

Lawrence Maximillian looked at me over his little rectangular glasses and grinned.

"I'm always sure."

He slapped a business card on Pearson's desk. "Next

time you want to question my client, you call me first. We'll arrange a time and place that's convenient for my client and his busy schedule. If I hear you've tried to interfere with my client's freedom again, I'll add harassment to the charges."

We walked right out of the police department, leaving Pearson and the desk sergeant staring, mouths wide open, looking like they'd been hit over their heads with baseball bats themselves.

CHAPTER 21

A sleek Lexus was sitting in the police station parking lot. Maximillian clicked his clicker and all the lights went on and the engine purred to life.

"Get in."

"I still got my bike."

Maximillian sized up the bike. "It'll fit."

He popped the trunk and handed me his briefcase. He hefted the bike and popped it into the trunk, easy as pie, and then we were both in the car and starting to drive.

"Buckle up, Rabi."

We hit the highway, and he opened up the engine. We flew down the road. Inside the car, everything was glowing green with all the fancy GPS and computer stuff, speed dials, and audio controls on the steering wheel.

Maximillian tapped the stereo and something with thumping bass came on. Reggaeton. The kind of music my mom wouldn't let me listen to because she said it didn't treat women right. But the beat was full of awesome.

Maximillian grinned as I started to bob my head to the beat. "Feels good to stick it to the man, doesn't it?"

"Yeah. They wouldn't stop bothering me."

"Cops are like that."

He drove fast, and being inside the car, with its smooth ride, it felt like we were flying. It felt like we were in a completely different universe, where everything was sleek and rich and perfect.

Money.

Joe would have said it was *money*. Everything about Maximillian was money. Gold glinting watch. Not afraid of anyone. Bulldog lawyer, and he really knew how to bite.

We pulled up in front of my house. "How'd my mom find out about me?" I asked.

Maximillian shrugged. "Doesn't matter. The important thing is that we got you out of there."

"Is she mad?"

"Of course not. She just wants to make sure you're okay."

"She's not mad at all?"

Maximillian laughed. "Boys will be boys," he said. "Is Miguel here?"

"How'd you know about him?"

"Because in my line of work, you don't face down the police unless you've done your research. He's why the police were hassling you. Anyway, I'll need to speak with both of you."

"About ICE?" I asked. "Can you help him find his aunt and uncle?"

Maximillian shook his head. "Let's not rush into anything. He's not my client. We'll just have to see what his situation is and see what we can do to help. My firm doesn't specialize in immigration issues. We're more focused."

We both got out. "So what do you want to talk to us about?" I asked.

"There's a reason you went to the police in the first place."

"The zombies?"

"Bingo." He popped the trunk and got my bike out. "Go see if Miguel is here. We have a lot to discuss."

I went up and unlocked the door. The house was pitch-black. I found Miguel hiding in a back room, in a closet. When I came in, he said, "Oh man, I'm sure glad it's you."

"What's the matter?"

"The cops came by, knocking on the door. I saw them through the curtains and didn't answer, but they were here."

"Don't worry," I said. "We got a lawyer."

"We do?"

I led him out to the living room and introduced him to Lawrence Maximillian. Maximillian shook Miguel's hand seriously, and then guided us all into the kitchen. "It's very good to meet you, Miguel. Rabi seems quite concerned about your situation." He went and got a couple of root beers from the fridge for us. Cracked them open and had us all sit down at the kitchen table.

"All right," he said. "Why don't you tell me about what happened to you out in the cornfields." He got out a thin little laptop from his briefcase. "Start from the beginning. The first moment when you started to think that something might be wrong."

So we did. We talked and he typed and his little glasses glowed blue with the reflected light off his laptop screen. He typed and typed and typed. It felt great to finally find a real responsible adult.

Talking with all the other grown-ups had been like talking to a brick wall. But Lawrence Maximillian was different. The guy really listened. He didn't make jokes or act like we weren't real people or talk down to us. He looked us in the eye, and listened, and wrote everything down.

We told him what we'd heard from Miguel's uncle and aunt, about the weird things they were feeding the cows at the plant and the weird drugs they were giving them, and all the stuff about how bad it smelled out there the day we'd been playing at Milrow Park, and then about Mr. Cocoran and the other zombie that we'd also seen, and how there might be more of them around. And Lawrence Maximillian listened.

We told him about how we took everything out of Miguel's house, and how we ditched the truck out by Milrow, and how Miguel couldn't find his passport, so we didn't know if he'd get grabbed and deported, or if he'd be able to stay, or if we could trust anyone.

Finally, we ran out of stuff to say.

Mr. Maximillian straightened and smiled. He pulled another machine out of his briefcase, sort of unfolded it, and then he started feeding paper into it, page after page, printing out all the stuff that we'd said.

"This is wonderful, gentlemen," he said. "Really useful. Do you have any photos or other evidence that I should see? Sometimes young people have cell phones—maybe you snapped pictures? Souvenirs?"

We both looked at each other. "Joe has a cell," I said. "But we didn't think to use it."

"That's fine. Not a problem at all. That's just fine. This is all very useful."

"Can you help Miguel with ICE?"

"We should be able to make an arrangement so that he's protected here in the United States. ICE will back off, if there's enough pressure, and my firm and our partner firms can provide that sort of pressure. But it's very important that you understand how hard it is to fight agencies like ICE. They're drunk on their own power. Luckily, they roll over like puppies if the right senator gives them a call. With us in your corner, ICE will never know what hit them."

He looked grave. "But I should also tell you that this is a very serious thing. A zombie uprising isn't something that anyone wants in the news. Panic. Fear. Lost business." He pushed the papers across to us. "I'll need you both to sign these."

I hesitated. My dad and mom always said you shouldn't sign anything without knowing what it was.

"What's this?"

"A standard NDA. A nondisclosure agreement. It states that your testimony on the issues related to untoward occurrences and certain other pieces relevant to the appearance of what people might call a 'zombie uprising' is proprietary trade information. A business secret that cannot be reported to others without legal repercussions."

We both must have looked confused, because he said, "It's a promise to keep the zombies a secret."

"But why would we do that? Don't people need to know something's going wrong out at Milrow?"

"Two reasons. One, my firm can't do anything about the problem unless you swear to keep it a secret. Two, we can't help Miguel with ICE unless we have your full cooperation." He smiled again, all friendly-like, but for the first time I wasn't totally convinced that Maximillian was actually a friend.

In fact, the more I thought about it, the more I realized that Lawrence Maximillian was a total stranger.

He might have looked like Spider Jerusalem, but that didn't mean he *was* Spider Jerusalem. The guy had suddenly popped into our lives, out of nowhere. He'd walked right into my house, and he'd acted all friendly, like he belonged, but he didn't really. And keeping the zombies a secret didn't seem right, and the way he talked about

Miguel and ICE didn't, either. The more he talked, the more wrong he seemed.

"Who are you working for?" I asked.

Maximillian grinned. "Just think of me as the cleanup squad."

"Cleanup squad? So...you're not working for my mom, or us, or anything like that?"

"I'm afraid not. But we'd really like your help on this," Maximillian said. "And of course, if you're helping us, then we have a good reason to make sure nothing *unfortunate* happens to Miguel. We all know how precarious it is, living in this country without any documentation at all."

This guy had gotten root beers out my fridge. He'd been so smooth about it that I hadn't even noticed. I'd just started drinking the root beer he'd given me, like he was the host, and I was the guest. It was creepy how smooth he'd been.

"Are you saying you're going to get me deported if I don't sign these papers?" Miguel asked.

"Of course not. That would be impossible. You're a good American citizen, aren't you? You haven't broken any laws. You're a model of virtue. Why would ICE care about you?"

Maximillian shuffled his papers, read something, and circled it with a red pen. "But perhaps you want help ... well, for whatever reasons you might want it ... for yourself, for your family, perhaps ... My firm and our partners can't fight ICE on your behalf, if you don't sign. You can certainly go it alone." He shrugged. "Sometimes people win." He looked up from his papers. "But let's be honest. The specifics of your case aren't exactly to your advantage, are they, Miguel?"

Miguel turned guarded. "I don't know what you're talking about."

"Come now, Miguel. Let's stop the charade. I know your situation. I know. Every. Single. Detail."

The blood had gone out of Miguel's face. He was practically as pale as Joe, all of a sudden.

"What's he talking about?" I asked.

Miguel just looked horrified. "Who hired you?"

"That's not the question you should ask." Maximillian pulled his cell phone out and laid it on the table beside him. "The only question you should ask is who I can call on this phone. Some of the numbers in this phone can help you. Others?" He shrugged. "Not so much."

Miguel was looking more and more afraid.

Maximillian went on. "You have so many enemies, boy. And we both know how they'll treat you if they catch you. For someone in your situation, the border is just a phone call away."

"You can't do anything to Miguel!" I said. "He's American. You can't do anything to him. We'll find his passport, or his birth certificate, or something! The hospital will have it. You can't do anything to him. He can't be deported."

"Miguel?" Maximillian asked.

I looked from Miguel to Maximillian. It was like they were having a secret conversation through telepathy or something. Like in Joe's comics. Like Professor X, or M'gann M'orzz and J'onn J'onzz being able to read each other's minds. And I was completely shut out of whatever it was that they were actually saying.

The one thing I could tell was that Miguel looked more scared than anyone I'd ever seen.

"We should sign," Miguel said. "Just sign, Rabi."

CHAPTER 22

"Are you serious?" I looked from Miguel to Maximillian. "This guy isn't our friend. Who knows what's in these papers?"

"It doesn't matter," Miguel said. "Just sign it, Rabi."

"Listen to your friend, Rabi." Maximillian beamed. "It's so much better when we're all cooperating. This way, we all get what we want."

Maximillian was slicker than snot. Nasty and slippery and totally out for himself. I couldn't believe I'd trusted him for even a second. I'd been so stupid.

Maximillian offered us pens. "Let's get these papers signed, and I'll be on my way."

"Who do you work for?" I asked again. "Who told you about us?"

"Does it really matter? Maybe the police talk too much on their radios. Maybe your neighbors talk too much about boys who are up to strange things. Maybe there are eyes and ears all around you, and you don't even know it. Focus on your friend, Rabi. All you need to worry about is how to protect Miguel, and how you're going to stay very, very quiet about all of this."

"Milrow," I guessed suddenly. "You work for Milrow Meats, and you want to cover all this up."

"It doesn't matter," Miguel said, signing furiously. "Just sign it, Rabi."

I'd never seen Miguel back down from anything in his life. But now it was like he didn't have a bit of fight in him.

"What's the matter with you?" I said. "We can't let this guy push us around."

Miguel shoved the papers over to Maximillian, and he looked so scared and sad and unhappy....

I finally got it.

I finally understood why Miguel was so scared of ICE, and the reason Lawrence Maximillian could just lean on him and expect him to crumple.

"Miguel?" I said. "You *were* born here, weren't you?"

Miguel wouldn't meet my eyes. He gave a shrug—kind of sad, kind of sorry, kind of giving up.

"Sorry, Rabi."

He wasn't American at all.

I mean, he *was* American, you know? We'd grown up together, and did all the stuff like Little League, and making bike jumps over creeks, and taking allowance money down to Casey's to buy root beers... but he wasn't *American* American. He was one of the people all the politicians kept screaming about on the news. The illegals. The ones who were supposed to be taking everyone's jobs and spreading crime or whatever. And here he was, sitting at the kitchen table, looking run over by Lawrence Maximillian.

"My parents brought me here when I was just a little baby," Miguel said. "I never had a birth certificate here in America."

Maximillian looked like a satisfied lizard, sitting at my kitchen table and smiling.

"There's nothing I can do," Miguel said. "If he calls ICE..." He made a slicing motion across his neck. "It's all over for me."

Maximillian broke in. "It's not like that at all, Miguel. With friends like Rabi and Joe, you're in a much better position than you describe. Assuming all of you behave..."

"You mean you're blackmailing all of us to be quiet

about the zombies, or you'll do something to Miguel," I said.

"You make it sound so unpleasant. All we need is a signature and silence. We'll take care of the zombie question and you boys can go back to playing baseball and video games. No one needs to care about who was born when, or where. Everything can go back to normal." He tapped his phone, reminding us that disaster was just a phone call away. "What's it going to be, Rabi?"

What was I going to do? Maximillian could just call ICE and Miguel would be kicked out of the country.

I signed.

I hated doing it, but I signed.

Maximillian whisked the papers out of my hands. "Very good choice, young man." Suddenly he was all friendly and smiling again. He looked at Miguel. "We have a partner firm who will be in touch with you about your immigration concerns. We're very good at protecting people we care about."

He pulled a box out of his briefcase and popped it open. "As you'll be on your own until Rabi's mother comes back, you'll probably need some spending money." He pulled out a wad of bills and started laying cash out on the table. My jaw hit the floor. The bills were hundreds.

He counted out $500 for each of us. Fanned the cash open, stacked it, and handed it across with a flourish. "Well done, gentlemen. Well done." He snapped his briefcase closed and headed for the door.

Just before he left, he turned back to us. "Remember, gentlemen. Not a word of this. Not a single word to anyone. Or Miguel is on his own."

"We get it," I said.

"Of course you do, but let me make it clear. If you tell your friends or your parents or some policeman or a reporter, or you Tweet it or Facebook it or Tumblr it, or blog or blab on whatever new Web toy you use these days, then the full force of this agreement will come into effect. My firm is very good at lawsuits. By the time we are done with you, you will have no home, no money, your parents will have no jobs, and Miguel will have no future."

He went back to smiling, quick as a blink. "A pleasure, gentlemen. Let's hope we never have occasion to meet again."

And then he was gone, out the door and down the walk. His Lexus purred to life, little lights blinking. The car pulled out and whooshed off.

Lawrence Maximillian: the face of evil.

As soon as he was gone, I punched Miguel in the shoulder. "You should have told me!" I said. "I would've had your back!"

"Ow! My mom and dad said I shouldn't talk about it."

"But this is me! You think you can't trust me? We grew up together! You think I'm some kind of rat? I wouldn't call ICE!"

"It's not like that, Rabi. I didn't even know until a couple years ago. My mom and dad didn't even tell me."

"Oh, so you've only kept it a secret for a couple of years."

"Don't be like that. If word got around, I'd be in deep trouble. It doesn't matter if someone tells on purpose, or not. All that matters is if people know about me, then I got ICE breathing down my neck."

"But still, you should've told *me*," I said. "I thought I was your best friend!"

"This isn't a game, Rabi! This is my life! This isn't about all the kid stuff like cross your heart and hope to die." Miguel was mad now. "My whole family's gone. You don't got to worry about this stuff, but I do! If I make one mistake, they're going to dump me in some country I never even seen before. My Spanish is more like Spanglish! I wanted to tell you a million times. A billion! But I couldn't risk it. And now you have to keep the secret, too. You got to swear."

"Of course I swear. I would've sworn a million years ago! And I wouldn't have leaked."

"You got to swear," Miguel said again, and his voice was fierce. "You got to swear!"

I grabbed his shoulders and looked him in the eye. "I swear. I won't tell anyone. Never, never, never. I swear on my mother's grave."

"Swear on Ganesha."

"Okay! I swear on Ganesha and Lakshmi and Krishna!"

"Yeah. Okay." Miguel hesitated. "You swear?"

"I already did. Stop being a jerk. I wouldn't have told then, and I won't tell now. Quit insulting me."

I was trying not to show how much it hurt to find out that he hadn't trusted me all along. Miguel knew everything about me. He even knew about the time I peed the bed in third grade, and I hadn't even told Joe that, because I knew Joe would have made fun of me for weeks. But Miguel had been keeping a huge secret from me. And even now, I could tell that he was still worried about me knowing.

I changed the subject. "So that lawyer guy is what Milrow's like, huh?"

"Yeah. Milrow Meats. They play for keeps."

It almost sounded like an ad slogan: *Milrow Meats. We play for keeps.*

At another time, it might have seemed funny. But after meeting that cold-blooded lizard named Lawrence Maximillian, it mostly felt like an understatement.

CHAPTER 23

It turned out that Maximillian the lizard lawyer had gone to visit Joe, too, and he'd done the same thing to Joe that he did to us. Acted all nice, then turned mean when Joe started asking questions.

Joe signed the papers, too.

The next day, we all sat on our bikes, staring at the Milrow meatpacking complex. Steam rose from the chimneys, and the normal nasty smells of manure and rot billowed off the feedlots, joined by the mooing of the cows.

Something had happened there, but now nobody was supposed to talk about it. It was going to be a secret forever.

"That place took my whole family," Miguel said. "It

just ate them up. Ground them up and threw them away when they weren't useful."

"They aren't eaten up," I said. "They're down in Mexico. They'll figure out a way to come back to you."

Miguel shook his head. "Coming across the border isn't like it used to be. My dad said it was easy when he came across. Nobody minded so much if you wanted to come over and work hard. Nobody watched the border much, back then." He shrugged. "Now they got all kinds of Border Patrol and army down there.... It's dangerous now."

"That's okay," Joe said. "We got all this cash from Milrow. You can hire one of those guys who guides people across."

"Coyotes," Miguel said.

"Yeah. Them. You can hire a coyote. With all this money we got you can hire a good one." He reached into his pocket and pulled out the wad of bills, but Miguel wasn't looking at it. He was still looking at Milrow.

"Money," Miguel said. "I can't believe I took their money."

"You didn't have a choice," I said.

Miguel's jaw clenched at that. "You always got a choice. Just sometimes you don't like the choices you got. But you always got a choice. And I chickened out and took Milrow's money, all because I was scared of being kicked out of the country."

"Yeah, well, I was scared you were going to get kicked out, too," I said. "We all took the money. Not just you. No way I was going to be the guy who got you kicked out."

"Me, either," Joe said.

When Joe found out that Miguel didn't have his citizenship, his reaction had been to laugh about it, and then to be impressed at all the ways Miguel and his parents had been fooling the system. He'd hardly been bothered at all that Miguel had kept his situation secret for so long. I asked Joe about it later, about why he wasn't bothered about the lying, and he just looked at me like I was crazy.

"It's like Miguel's secret identity, right? You don't see Spider-Man or Superman giving away their secret identities. Batman? You got to be kidding. Some secrets are too dangerous to share."

"Yeah, but even they've got *some* real friends."

"This is the biggest secret in the whole world," Joe said. "But it's *Miguel's* secret. If you're going to be his *real* friend, you keep it to yourself, and you don't complain about whether he told you before. You step up and prove that you were worthy all along. That's what a real friend does. You step up. You get it?"

I kind of did. And I was kind of impressed, too, because Joe wasn't the kind of guy you expected to hear that stuff from. He could fool you with all his joking and craziness and bad grades. You could think you knew him because of the way he acted on the outside, but then inside, he was completely different.

Joe was still talking to Miguel, coming up with ideas to help. "Maybe we could get your parents, like, night-vision goggles and stuff, so they can come across easier. There's this whole website we can get stuff like that on, and then we could ship it down and they could be like ninjas and sneak across."

Well, not *completely* different. He was still bugnuts.

"You think Maximillian will actually try to help you stay here?" I asked Miguel. "Or was he just saying that stuff?"

"Now that we signed those papers?" Miguel shrugged. "I bet ICE shows up any second, and I'm needing Joe's ninja gear, too."

Joe leaned against his handlebars. "I don't get what people think you're supposed to do in Mexico. It's not fair to send you off to some place you never lived in your life."

Miguel laughed. "You think ICE cares about fair? All they care about is that I don't look white and I don't

161

got papers. Heck, if I lived in Alabama or Arizona or any of those nutball states with the anti-foreigner laws, they probably would have just grabbed me off the street." He glanced over at me. "Probably, they'd grab you, too, Rabi. You look kind of brown yourself. I'd totally deport you."

"Thanks, man."

"Just sayin'. If your mom lived in Arizona...*Shhooooo!* She'd be gone before you knew it. Driving While Brown. That's a criminal offense down there. A cop would pull her over and ask for her papers and the next thing you knew, she'd be in jail."

"Now you're just talking crazy," Joe said. "It's not that bad. Nobody's going to just grab you for no reason."

"What do you mean, no reason? She's brown, isn't she? She talks with that funny Indian accent, doesn't she? You might not have to worry about this stuff, because you look like an American," Miguel said. "Me and Rabi? We need some camouflage."

"We should dye our hair blond," I said. "Then we'd totally blend in."

"Totally," Miguel said. "Surfer style."

"In Iowa?" Joe asked.

"Why not? You think I can't be a surfer? I'll get me a

surfboard and be, like, crazy California. One hundred percent pure American surfer."

"It would help if you lived near an ocean," I said.

"If I was going to dye my hair, I'd go green," Joe said.

Miguel gave him an incredulous look. "*Green?* They'd shoot you for being an alien, for sure, then."

"Or a leprechaun," I said.

"I got it." Miguel snapped his fingers. "Red, white, and blue. That would do the trick. ICE wouldn't come near me then."

We all started laughing, imagining red, white, and blue hair like the Fourth of July.

"Sparklers!" Joe said. "You could have sparklers, like, in your ears or something."

"Now you're just talking crazy. Next thing you know, you'd put me on stilts, too."

"ICE wouldn't even see you! They'd walk between your legs!"

After all the bad stuff that had been going on, it was good to laugh.

But when the laughing was done, Milrow Meat Solutions was still sitting there with its big old meatpacking plant and all its feedlots, and the mystery of whatever had gone wrong. Miguel's face turned grim again.

"I shouldn't have taken the money," Miguel repeated. "That lawyer guy made me afraid, but I shouldn't have taken his money. That's how they always do it. Trying to keep people afraid."

"Let it go," I said. "We should get to baseball practice."

"Are they even having it?" Miguel asked.

"I doubt Mr. Cocoran is going to be up for coaching, that's for sure," Joe said.

"Yeah, well, let's go find out," I said, not liking the way Miguel kept staring at Milrow. "It's not smart for us to be hanging around here, anyway." I nodded at a guy who was over by the doors of the Milrow building. He was looking right at us. "We don't want them to think we're going to make trouble."

I kept pulling at Miguel, and finally he let us drag him away. I didn't like the way he resisted, though. It was almost like he was starting to get his old fight back, except this time it was the kind of fight that he could only lose. The sooner he forgot about Milrow, the better.

We pedaled back down the highway, talking about other things, random things, but I couldn't help thinking back to what Miguel had said at Milrow, about needing to look like you fit in. Like you belonged.

If Joe had been the biggest illegal border-hopping ninja in the world, no cop in a million years would ask to see his passport or his green card or his immigration papers, because Joe had blond hair and pale skin. That was what an American was supposed to look like.

All Miguel wanted was to be left alone, but people were all lining up to take a whack at "the immigration problem" or "be tough on immigration"—and that meant Miguel was basically a real small baseball in a game where everyone wanted to take a real big swing.

* * *

When we got to the baseball field, it turned out Joe was right about practice. A bunch of kids were leaving as we skidded our bikes to a stop.

Andy, our first baseman, came by. "Practice is canceled."

"Yeah?"

"Cocoran's sick or something."

"So what're those guys doing?" Joe asked.

Andy looked over his shoulder. "It's Sammy. Him and some other guys are waiting for you, Miguel." He looked at us. "You really made him mad about something."

I guess it's not all that surprising that between the zombies and the ICE raid and lizard Maximillian, I'd completely forgotten our fight with Sammy at his house.

Andy said, "He's looking for payback. All he's talking about is how you and Rabi are toast." Andy slapped Miguel on the back. "I'd get out of here if I were you."

Across the baseball field, Sammy and his buddies had caught sight of us. Even from a distance, you could tell they were smiling. My stomach dropped into my shoes. No way was this going to turn out good.

They started toward us.

I tugged Miguel's sleeve as he straddled his bike. "Andy's right. Let's roll out of here," I said. "We don't want trouble."

But Miguel was watching Sammy, and he had the same expression on his face as he'd had back at Milrow— the look he got when he was about to step up.

"Miguel?" I said. "Let's go, man."

"Nah. I think I'm done running."

"If we go out there, they're going to kick our butts," Joe said.

"Guess we got to kick theirs first, then."

Joe nodded slowly, seeming to digest this. "Okaaaay. Final stand, huh?"

"Something like that."

One on one, Miguel could probably take Sammy and send that boy home crying. But Sammy had six of his biggest friends with him now: Travis Thompson, Sid Meacham, Rob Ziegler, Bart Lewis, Dale Toomey, and Otis Andrews. I could practically see the stats of doom over their heads.

Instead of batting averages and on-base percentages, I was seeing number of punches to knockout and health counters that went off the charts. Our own stats didn't add up—no way, no how.

Bart Lewis, all on his own, had a reputation for pounding. I'd run into him once by accident, coming around a corner in the school, and he'd just slammed me up against the lockers—*wham!*—and kept on walking.

"Miguel," I said, "they're going to wipe us all over the dirt."

"I'm not running."

"So call it a strategic retreat," I said. "Let's get Sammy some other time. We'll get him when he's not with his goons."

"If I run, I just keep running. All the time. They like us running and staying quiet. Ducking down, taking it. That's how they want us. They want us to be afraid."

" 'They?' " I asked, with a sinking feeling. "It's just

Sammy and his goons. There's no 'they.' It's not like this is a conspiracy or something."

Miguel shook his head. "There's always someone like Sammy who thinks we should back away. If it's not Sammy, it's his dad, or that Milrow lawyer, or it's some foreman out at the meatpacking plant telling people they should shut up and keep working and be grateful they got a job. It's always the same. Maybe they let you live, but you can't respect yourself. Lying low doesn't do any good. It just lets bad people think they can do bad things to you. Keep quiet, or stand tall, it doesn't matter. End of the day, they just keep coming after you."

"They've got baseball bats," I said.

"We do, too."

"This is insane!" I said. "Let's just get the heck out of here."

"You can go," Miguel said. "I don't mind. This isn't your fight."

I sure wanted to run. But I knew I'd hate myself forever if I ran off and left Miguel behind. With a sinking feeling, I realized that I was in this fight with him, no matter how stupid it was.

Joe was looking wild-eyed. "This is going to be so epic." He got off his bike and stood by Miguel.

It was stupid to fight when you were going to lose.

There was no way we could beat these guys. But it was like Miguel didn't care. Losing didn't mean the same thing to me that it did to him: For me, it was getting a pounding. For him, it was backing down.

I muttered my worst Bengali curse as I got off my bike and joined up with my friends. "Let's go, then."

We met Sammy and his goons halfway across the baseball field. Sammy stared down his bruised nose at Miguel.

"I figured you'd be in Mexico by now."

"I decided to stick around."

"You don't get to decide. We decide."

"Not when someone stands up to you." Miguel grinned. "Then you run for the porch like a little baby."

"I'm going to kill you."

"Not if I kill you first."

I started to worry that we weren't just talking about getting a whipping. Miguel and Sammy didn't like each other. I mean, *really* didn't like each other.

"Come on, guys," I said. "Let's not do this."

"Afraid?" Sammy taunted.

I looked at him, thinking, *Yes.* But I said, "No."

"Sure you are. How 'bout you go run back to that red-dot mommy of yours?"

"How about you shove off before we kick your teeth in?" Joe said.

The other boys all laughed at that. I knew them all. They weren't bad guys, mostly. But with Sammy, it was like they just stopped thinking. Like they couldn't remember that we'd gone to birthday parties together when we were little. That their little brothers or sisters had been our friends. It was like, as they grew up, they turned into something else.

"Go back where you came from," Sammy said.

"I came from here," I said. "Born and raised."

"Stupid Indian." He made a fake-y kind of war whoop with his hand over his mouth. "Wa wa wa wa wa."

"Wrong Indian, jerkwad."

"Oh, right, you're the ones who wear the towels on your heads."

I wanted to do that whole Gandhi thing where you don't resort to violence, I really did. I'm not a fighter, and I knew that if we started swinging that we'd get creamed.

Sammy smirked at me like he owned me.

So I socked him. Right in the nose. *Wham!*

Sammy howled. "Owwwwww!" and doubled over clutching his face as blood spurted from his nose.

I have to admit, for a second, it felt so great to pound him.

Everyone was staring at me, as amazed as I was that

I'd unloaded the first punch. But then I noticed that Miguel and Joe were looking worried, and so was everyone else. I realized suddenly that maybe this fight hadn't had to happen after all. Maybe everyone had been as afraid of fighting as I'd been, but now it was too late, and Sammy was howling mad.

CHAPTER 24

"I'm going to kill you!"

Sammy charged.

Cue replay of the fight on Sammy's lawn, only this time, Sammy had the advantage of numbers. I tried to make a run for it, but Sammy snagged me and then he started pounding. A tornado of punches. I hit the ground. Sammy jumped on top of me, whaling away.

Joe jumped on Sammy's back and Miguel gave him a kick and then the other guys piled in, too. And just like I'd known, there were too many of them and they were way too big. I couldn't get Sammy off me. Dale Toomey had grabbed my legs and was holding me down while Sammy pounded.

Miguel got free of Bart Lewis and charged in to

help me. He got one good hit on Sammy and then a bunch of the other guys grabbed him and started beating on him like bongo drums. Miguel knew a little wrestling, and I saw him flip Travis Thompson right onto his back, but the others were too much for him. Sammy gave me a final kick and left me to Dale, so he could go after Miguel.

I kicked free from Dale's grip and scrambled out of the dirt, trying to stay clear as he came after me again. Not far away, Otis Andrews had Joe down on the ground and was rubbing his face back and forth in the dirt.

"How you like that dirt wash?! You like eating dirt? You like that?"

Joe's face was all muddy and spitty and bloody.

I felt terrible, and not just because I was getting the stuffing beat out of me.

I'd done this. My punch had started it. I'd been trying to get Miguel to not fight, and then I'd ended up jumping right into the middle of it.

Had there been some other way out?

Running away sure would have been smarter.

Sammy and a couple of the other guys had Miguel down, and they were kicking him every time he tried to get up. He looked terrible.

I wanted to cry, but there wasn't anything to do

except keep fighting. It was either keep fighting or curl up and bawl, and I didn't think they'd stop, even then.

We were toast.

And that's when I saw the cow.

It was at the top of the little hill overlooking the baseball field where the bleachers were, and where families would sometimes spread out blankets to watch the game.

The cow was just kind of standing there, looking confused and dizzy. It staggered a little, then got its footing again, almost like it was drunk.

At first, I thought I was hallucinating because of the fight and the pain, but then that cow looked at us, and I swear it looked hungry.

It started down the hill, stumbling and unsteady, but gathering speed. A big lumbering freight train of a cow, barreling straight for us.

What the...?

The cow gave a weird groan, low and then rising. And then again, louder: "MMMMOOOOOOooooooooooo!"

Everyone else was so busy fighting that they didn't notice. Miguel was still getting kicked, and Joe was still getting wiped.

"MMMMMOOOOOOOOOOOooooooo!"

Uh-oh.

As it charged down the hill, I realized what was coming for us:

Zombie cow.

A thousand pounds of undead bovine threat, scratched and beat-up and leaking blood, and it was coming right for us.

I tore away from Dale Toomey and tackled Otis, dragging him off Joe. Joe got up to boot him, but I grabbed him and shoved him around, pointing.

"Look!"

Joe's eyes widened at the charging animal. Otis was coming back at us, but I waved him off. "We're done! You win!" Praying that he'd listen. Otis wasn't all bad. At least when Sammy wasn't around.

Otis stopped for a second. "You win!" I said again. Otis grabbed Dale and held him off. I pointed at the cow behind them. "We all better get out of here."

Otis turned and gaped at the charging cow. "What the—"

But I wasn't waiting to see what Otis did next. Joe and I dove into the fight, where the other five guys were kicking the stuffing out of Miguel. We got hold of our buddy and dragged him out.

Miguel was bloody and scraped, but he was still

spoiling to get back into the fight. "Come on!" he shouted. "I'll take you all on! I'm not afraid!"

The cow was coming. I could actually feel the ground shaking. I yanked Miguel around and pointed. "Zombie cow!" I shouted as it crashed toward us. "Run!"

Miguel finally got it. We ran for our lives.

Behind us, the older boys laughed.

Well, they laughed for a second.

CHAPTER 25

I thought I heard Otis and Dale shouting at their friends to shut up and run, and then all I heard was screaming and the craziest, loudest mooing in the world.

I looked back.

The cow had grabbed Bart Lewis by the arm and was shaking him around the way a dog shakes a rat with its teeth.

All the other boys were beating on the cow with their bats, but it was huge, and it didn't seem to notice at all. With a final shake of its head, the cow tore off a chunk of Bart's arm, and Bart flew through the air. We winced as the cow gulped down the flesh and went after the other guys.

"Should we go back?" Joe asked.

"No way," I said. "No way we can fight a cow with just our bats."

"But cows are stupid and slow. We should be able to chase it off."

"Not that one."

And it was true. That cow wasn't calm and stupid like the normal cows we'd grown up around. Watching that zombie cow, you could see why old-time cowboys feared cattle stampedes. Cows were fast when they wanted to be. And a zombie cow...well, it was vicious, too.

A bunch of the guys were sprinting for the far side of the field now, chased by the zombie cow.

Bart lay where he'd landed in the field. Otis separated from the other five and ran over to Bart.

"This doesn't look good." I got on my bike and rode into the baseball diamond, to Otis. He knelt over Bart. As I got close, he looked up at me, eyes wide with shock.

"Sorry about your friend," I said as I came to a stop.

Otis was patting Bart's face. "He's okay," he said. "He's going to be okay." He stared after the zombie cow. It had disappeared off the field, chasing Sammy and the other three boys. "What was that all about?"

"It's a zombie cow," I said.

"Right."

"Seriously. I'm not making it up. And you should get

away from Bart. He's going to be a zombie soon, too. You should probably run."

"He's my friend."

"Not anymore. Now he's a zombie."

"I still got to help him."

I looked down at Bart. He lay there, moaning. I'd never liked Bart much, because he was so mean, but I kind of felt bad for Otis, losing a friend like this. If it had been Miguel or Joe, it would have killed me.

"Look," I said, "at least don't let him bite you, or you'll be a zombie, too. Seriously. Watch out for it. I'm not crazy and I'm not joking. If he turns weird, you got to keep him from biting you."

I got on my bike and pedaled back to my friends.

Joe scowled at me as I rejoined them. "Why'd you do that?"

I looked back at Otis. "He was the only one who fought fair."

"Do you see my face?" Joe pointed at the mud and blood and scraped skin. "He practically rubbed it off."

"Yeah. But he did it alone. And when we wanted to stop fighting, he didn't keep beating on us."

Miguel nodded. "Yeah. He's okay," he said. "Maybe he won't get bitten."

"Now what do we do?"

The cow came lumbering back to the baseball diamond, apparently having missed catching any other snacks. Otis grabbed Bart and threw him over his shoulders in a fireman's carry and stumbled off the field. I really hoped he was smart enough not to get himself bitten.

The cow staggered around the field, eating grass and then spitting it out like it didn't taste right.

"We've got to call the police," I said. "This time we've got a whole cow to show them. This is real evidence, now."

"You want to tangle with the cops again?" Miguel asked.

I thought about it. "They think I've got a big-time lawyer."

"That lawyer isn't our friend. He made us sign papers not to get involved and to stay quiet about all of this."

"Yeah, well, there's a zombie cow, right in the middle of the baseball field, so I don't think it's much of a secret."

"We could call it in anonymously," Joe said.

"That's better," Miguel agreed.

So we did.

And then we waited and watched.

CHAPTER 26

But instead of the cops showing up, what we saw was a big white truck and a couple of those rent-a-cop cars drive up, and a bunch of guys in heavy leather clothes get out.

They roped the cow right up with lassos and dragged it into the truck. And then more guys got out, and they cleaned up all the blood and dug up some patches of grass, taking away the last of the evidence.

"What do you want to bet that's Milrow Meats?" Miguel said.

"They're running around covering everything up?" Joe asked.

"Looks like it." I said. "But how'd they know where to go?"

Joe looked thoughtful. "My old man listens to police scanners. Maybe they heard it that way. We called in a mad cow, and they knew they were looking for zombie cows on the loose, so they knew right where to go."

"Didn't Maximillian say something like that when he came and got me out of jail, too? Something about the police talking all the time, or something?"

"He also said he had eyes everywhere," Miguel said.

"Kind of seems like he does."

The cleanup squad slammed its doors and zipped off.

A few minutes later a police car came by and tooled around the edge of the baseball field. Baby Face Boone, keeping us safe from nothing at all.

"You know this is just going to keep getting worse," I said.

"You mean Bart turning into a zombie?"

"And whoever else that cow bit. And whoever any other cows have bit. Milrow's probably got a ton of those zombie cows, by now."

Joe sort of grinned at that. "I wonder what would happen if those cows got turned into zombie burgers?"

"They'd never let that happen," I said.

Miguel looked at me and laughed. "Milrow Meats? You mean the guys who just deported my whole family? They'd do anything to make a buck."

"You really think they'd do something like that?" Joe asked. He had a light in his eyes that I didn't like—a look that said WOULDN'T IT BE COOL IF THE ZOMBIE APOCALYPSE HAPPENED, AND I GOT TO SMACK UNDEAD ALL DAY LONG?

"If it saved money, or made money, they'd do it for sure," Miguel said. "I'm pretty sure they called ICE on my uncle and every other worker there, and got them deported so no one could report any weirdness. Cash is king."

"Then we've got to tell the police..." I started to say. I stopped halfway into the sentence as we watched the police cruiser go around the loop again.

Miguel laughed. "There they are."

Miguel was right. The cops were idiots. Baby Face Boone wasn't going to save us from squat.

"So it's on us," I said. "We've got to find some proof that they can't ignore, and that Milrow can't cover up."

"Yeah!" Joe said. "Milrow meat raid! Throwdown! *Final Battle at the Zombie Meatpacking Plant!*"

"Dude. You read too many comics."

"They should do a *Left 4 Dead* in a meatpacking plant. I'd totally order that with my mom's credit card. It'd be worth getting grounded for."

"I'm not going," Miguel said suddenly.

I turned around, confused. "Why not?"

"Why should I?" he asked. He waved at the town. "Milrow already got rid of my family, and any day now, ICE is going to get hold of me...." He shrugged. "What's the point? Everyone's always telling me this isn't my country, and I don't belong. Good old Sammy, you know." Miguel touched his lip, which was fattening up from our fight. "If these people don't want me around, I don't see any reason to worry about them."

"Don't listen to Sammy," I said. "He's a jerk."

"Yeah, well, so's everyone on TV. And all those politicians running for office, saying how they're going to get tough on immigration, like they're going to get tough on some kind of rat infestation." He shrugged. "The heck with them. This is their zombie apocalypse. Not mine." He frowned. "Now that I think about it, maybe I wish I did get deported. I'll bet Mexico's totally safe. No way a zombie's going to be able to cross the border."

"Don't say that!"

"Why not? I'll be safe." He shrugged again. "Anyway, it's not my problem."

"Then why the heck did I stand up for you?" I said. "I just got completely pounded for you."

"If you want to come south, I'm okay with that. I think I'm going to Mexico, though. I'm done with America."

"Miguel," I said. "You're the only way we can get into the meatpacking plant."

"I already told you, I'm not going."

"Come on! It'll be cool!" Joe said. "I bet they got tons of zombie cow, and zombie steak, and zombie burger, and zombie intestines."

"Who eats intestines?" I asked.

Joe shrugged. "I dunno. But I bet someone does."

"I don't eat any of it," I said.

"Don't gimme that *Hindus don't eat cows* stuff," Joe said. "Burger is too good not to eat."

"Yeah." Miguel nodded. "Except for zombie burgers. Anyway, they grind up all the bits of intestines and tendons and stuff and turn it into this pink slime stuff that they pour back into the burgers. My uncle told me about it."

"That's nasty," Joe said. "I'm okay with zombie burgers, but pink slime? That's going too far."

"Okay, you guys," I said. "Seriously, we got to make some kind of plan."

"And like I said, I'm not going."

"Come on, Miguel! We can't just sneak into Milrow," I said. "It's locked. But your aunt and uncle used to go in and out all the time, right?"

Miguel looked stubborn. "I don't even know if the key's still in the house."

"So let's go find out."

"Why?"

Joe was looking at Miguel. "'Cause we aren't all like Sammy?"

There was a long pause. Miguel looked disgusted. "This better not get us killed."

"Trust me. I don't like it any better than you do."

"What if child services or ICE or someone is watching? They'll bust my butt."

"A second ago, you were planning on bailing to Mexico. Now you're worrying about ICE?"

Miguel looked down at the ground, then up at me. "I guess I owe you, for the fight. But unless you've got a plan to get into my house without ICE or the police or child services catching us, it still doesn't matter."

"No problem." I slapped Joe on the back. "That's why we got all-American Joe, here. No one cares what a nice blond good boy like this does, right?"

"I'm a good boy?" Joe asked, surprised.

"Today you are."

"Cool." He wiped his bloody nose on his arm. "Does that mean I have to clean up?"

* * *

Cleaning Joe took a while, because he'd managed to bleed all over his shirt and stuff, too. And then we had to sneak up to Miguel's house so we could scout it out. After about ten minutes of sneaking, we ended up peeking through a hedge across the street from Miguel's house.

"What do you think?" I asked Miguel as we surveyed the street through the bushes.

Two doors over, a dog was barking like a loon. I sure hoped it was fenced in, because I seriously didn't want it suddenly appearing and jumping on my back.

"Dunno. It looks empty, and I don't see anything suspicious."

"Are you ready for me to do my thing?" Joe asked.

He was freshly scrubbed and psyched to play All-American Good Boy. He'd tried to bring a slingshot, but I'd confiscated that from him.

"No weapons!"

"What am I supposed to do if I run into ICE?" Joe protested.

"Don't pick a fight, that's for sure," Miguel said.

"How come you're the only one who gets to pick fights?"

187

"'Cause I actually win," Miguel said. "Just get in there and see if anyone's around."

Joe went around the back, and a few minutes later he rode down the street on his bike, looking like some kid in a Norman Rockwell painting. He rolled up to the door and unlocked it. A second later he came out and waved for us.

"Guess nobody cares about a leftover Mexican kid," Miguel said, as we grabbed our bikes and shoved through the hedges.

The way he said it made me worry.

He didn't sound mad. It was more like he sounded lost.

I started to ask him what he meant by "nobody caring," but as we were rolling up the front walk, Miguel's nosy neighbor Mrs. Olsen came out.

She looked at us for a second, her face surprised.

"HEY!"

"Her? Again?" We dropped our bikes. Joe opened the door for us, and we all piled inside.

"Close the door!" I shouted.

But, of course, Joe was just standing there, sticking his tongue out at the lady instead.

"Get in here!" Miguel yanked Joe inside and slammed the door and locked it.

188

Mrs. Olsen started pounding. "I know you're in there!" she shouted.

"We know you're out there, too!" Joe shouted back.

Miguel smacked him upside the head. "Shut up, you idiot."

"Ow." Joe rubbed his head.

"Hurry up and find the key," I said.

The lady kept banging on the door. Miguel finally came back with a plastic card. "Got it!"

"That's the key? Is it going to work?" I asked.

"Sure," he said. "You just swipe it."

I looked at the card. "What if it's like a hotel key, and they turn it off when you check out?"

Miguel said, "Well, then you'll have to figure something else out, mastermind. This is what we got. You want to try using it, or not?"

"Yeah, yeah." I peered out the door's peephole. Mrs. Olsen was still out there, pacing back and forth.

"Uh-oh," I said.

"What?"

"Looks like she's calling someone on her cell."

"Should we go out the back?" Joe said.

Miguel shook his head. "She's got our bikes out there."

"Why's she got to butt in?" Joe scowled. "It's not even her business."

189

"You're the one who made faces at her," I pointed out.

"How're we going to get around without bikes?"

Miguel looked from me to Joe. "Forget this." He grabbed his baseball bat and opened the door. "I'll take care of it."

"Is he going to hit her?" Joe asked.

"Dunno."

But I was worried. Miguel was walking toward the lady fast, the bat loose in his hands. "Please get off my lawn, ma'am," I heard him say. "You're trespassing."

The woman took one look at him and bolted.

Heck, I would have been scared, too. Come to think of it, he was kind of a bigger guy than he used to be. A couple years ago, he would have looked like a bratty little kid. Now he looked like serious business.

Miguel waved at us. "Come on," he said. "She'll call the cops for sure now."

"Are you crazy?" Joe asked.

Miguel shrugged. "I'm already in trouble. I'm tired of worrying about it."

There it was—that weird tone of voice, again.

I didn't like the sound of it at all. It sounded like someone who had lost all hope and didn't care about consequences anymore.

It scared the heck out of me.

CHAPTER 27

We pedaled down the highway toward the meatpacking plant, thick green rows of corn blurring past on either side.

We sweated buckets.

"Do you think we'll see more of those zombie cows?" Joe asked.

"I sure hope not," I said.

"You got to admit that last one was pretty awesome, though."

"You might like the idea of living through the zombie apocalypse," I said, "but this is serious. The best thing that can happen is that Milrow will have everything fixed—they figure out the problem with their meat, and we just go back to living our regular lives."

Miguel snorted. "Don't count on it. I'll bet you a hundred of Larry Max's dollars that there's a whole pile of zombie cows running around out there, and Milrow isn't doing any fixing of anything."

"Larry Max?" Joe asked.

"The lawyer, right? Lawrence Maximillian. Larry Max."

"Larry Max." Joe nodded thoughtfully. "That's got a good ring to it. Like Duke Nukem. *Larry Max.* If he had a couple of bazookas, you could totally make him into a video game character."

I started imagining a combination of Nick Fury of S.H.I.E.L.D. and Spider Jerusalem: tons of muscles and tattoos, bald with shattered red-and-green glasses, smoking a cigar, and packing a pair of wide-barreled bazooka pistols that blew up cows.

It actually sounded kind of awesome. Joe was clearly thinking along the same lines. "Larry Max—Zombie Cow Killer," he boomed in his best deep movie voice. "I'd totally play that."

A car was coming up the highway.

"We'd better get off the road, Zombie Cow Killer," Miguel said. "Someone's bound to see us if we get much closer to the plant."

"Back in the corn?" Joe asked. "You remember what happened the last time?"

"Quit being a baby," Miguel said as he steered off the road. "I thought you liked hunting zombies."

"I at least want to see them coming!"

"Don't be a wimp," I said. "The only way we're going to learn anything is if we go around the back side of the plant, where the manure lakes are. That's where we saw the poop zombie attacking that cow."

"Plus, no one in their right mind would go near a sewer lagoon," Miguel said.

"Exactly. It's a perfect place to hide zombie cows."

"Rabi's going first, though, right?" Joe said.

"No. For that comment, you're the one who's going in first," I said.

"We're all going together," Miguel said, and grabbed Joe by the shirt and dragged him into the corn.

"Hey!"

But Joe didn't fight hard, and pretty soon, we were all hacking through the greenery, finding our way more by smell than anything else, gagging as we got closer and closer.

Eventually the lagoon appeared in front of us, a huge lake of liquid cow poop. On the far side, corrals stretched far into the distance, full of mooing cows.

"Well?" Joe said.

"We need to go around and get closer."

We started skirting the edge of the manure lagoon, trying to stay out of the muck and holding our breaths against the nauseating stench.

"How many cows you think they got out here?" Joe gasped.

"You do the math," I gagged. "If the average American eats x pounds of beef every week, and Milrow is supplying beef to seven states, which have a combined population of p...You end up with fifty-two times p times x pounds of beef per year, then you just have to divide that by the average weight of meat you can cut off a cow, call that m, and—"

"Forget it, I'd rather count."

It added up to thousands of cows, whichever method you used. We covered our faces with our shirts and kept working our way around the lagoon, headed for the corrals on the far side.

"Mr. Cocoran was the first zombie we saw, and he was around here. And then there was that other one—"

"Whoever that was."

"—so I'm thinking that the zombies probably started somewhere out here in the feedlots."

We got closer and closer to the corrals. The cows were jammed in like sardines. They stank and they were nasty, but...

"I don't see anything weird," Joe said.

"Keep looking," Miguel said.

We climbed up on one of the corral fences. Flies buzzed around the cows. Tails flicked. They were covered with poop and eating out of long troughs of grain. Cows as far as the eye—

"Whoa." There it was, buried in the middle of all the other cows. Another corral.

"Come on," Joe said. "Let's go take a look."

He jumped up on the fence and started balance-beaming along its edge. When Miguel and I hesitated, he laughed. "What? Just don't fall off."

I climbed up onto the fence rail with him, trying not to teeter. It gave me a good view across all the corrals, an even grid of fences separating one group of cows from the next for acres and acres. By following the fence lines, we could get deeper among the corrals and never have to get down with the cows. Joe took off and Miguel and I followed, carefully balancing along the wooden rails, looking down at all the mooing and stinking cows on both sides of us. I wondered what they would have paid to be us, up here on the fence rails, instead of stuck down there—

My foot slipped.

"Whoa!"

A hand grabbed me and steadied me out.

"Pay attention," Miguel said. "You'll get smushed down there. If you fall into a corral, some big old cow will stand on you and won't even notice he's doing it."

A few minutes later, we made it to the corral we'd seen from a distance, buried deep among all the other, more normal ones.

It was completely different from all the rest. This one seethed with hungry, angry cattle. They screamed and slammed into one another, fighting and biting. Instead of quietly shoving their faces into feed troughs, they circled and fought in the corral like schools of crazed sharks, showing milky-white eyes and blood-smeared mouths.

"Well, Joe," I said. "You got your zombie cows."

Joe was staring with awe. "Dang. There's a lot of them."

"You got your phone with you?"

"What?" Joe seemed dazed by the sight of something even more insane than his comic books. "Oh. Yeah." He fumbled in his pocket and came up with the phone. He fiddled with it and started snapping pics. Then he just turned it to RECORD and swept the camera over the cows. "We can totally YouTube this."

Joe zoomed in as a zombie cow tore into the flank of another. That one squealed and bit back. The other zombie cows bucked in response, setting off a chain reaction of biting and thrashing and feeding. It was like watching a pond full of starving alligators.

"Eat Milrow beef," Miguel said in a bright TV-commercial voice. "If it's good enough for our cows, it's good enough for you."

Even though it was horrifying to watch cows chewing on one another—or maybe because of it—we all cracked up.

We were so busy laughing that we were caught by complete surprise when a real zombie—I mean a *human* zombie—popped up in the middle of the zombie herd, like a manure-covered jack-in-the-box.

It whipped around to focus on us and bared its teeth hungrily.

"Gah! What's that doing there? Sleeping?"

"BRAAAAAIiiiiiinnnsssss!" the zombie howled. It started trying to climb over the cows.

We made a move to run, but then remembered we were all standing on a four-inch-wide rail of fence, five feet above the ground. We started balance-beaming along the fence as fast as we could—which wasn't very fast.

"Hurry hurry hurry!" I knew the zombie was going to catch us at this rate.

"Hey, where'd the zombie go?" Miguel asked.

I spared a glance into the zombie cow corral. The pop-up zombie had disappeared into the herds again. It was creepy. One second it had been there, now it was gone. All that was visible was a sea of cows. It was almost like I'd imagined seeing it—

"GNAAAARR!" The zombie bounced up right beside us and lunged for our legs.

"Jack-in-the-box zombie!" Joe shouted as he danced madly, trying to keep from being yanked down into the corral.

"Get going!" I shouted as we danced and hopped and skipped, and the zombie made grabs for our legs. It was like some kind of Dance Dance Revolution game, trying to dodge the zombie's swiping hands. *Jump, land, forward, back, skip dodge, shuffle forward...*

The zombie swiped at my ankles. I jumped its swing and landed, barely balancing. It swiped again. "Whoa!" I back-shuffled and kept going. I was getting good at this. I could actually see when it wound up for a swing, so I could plan—

My foot slipped. "AAAAHHHHHhhh!" I piled over the side.

"*Rabi!*" Miguel and Joe shouted.

I landed in manure. All around me, cows started backing and shoving away as I climbed to my feet. At least I hadn't landed in the zombie corral.

Jack-in-the-box zombie glared at me through the fence. It banged against the barrier a couple of times, then tried to jam its head through the rails. It was a lot feistier than Mr. Cocoran had been.

"*Gaarrghghg!*" it growled.

We both stared at each other. The zombie bared its teeth and drooled. "*Brrraaainnsss.*" It jammed its arm through the rails, clawing for me.

I backed out of reach and ran smack into the side of a cow. The cow bolted and ran into its buddy, and that one bumped into another cow, and suddenly all the cows were freaking out—a huge sloshing wave of panicking cows, each one slamming up against the next, all of them looming over me.

"*Get out of there!*" Joe yelled. "You're going to get crushed!"

"I can't! This stupid zombie..."

The zombie grabbed for me again. There was no way I could climb the fence with it standing guard. I wished I had my baseball bat. I totally would have socked it.

"Use the other fence!"

A cow bashed into me, hurling me toward the zombie. I barely dodged snatching hands. As I leaped back from the zombie, searching for an escape, I got trapped between two more cows. Hot hairy hides smashed me, pressing tighter and tighter.

"*Uhgh…*" I couldn't breathe. My ribs felt like they were going to crack. I realized I was going to be smushed to death by a bunch of dumb cows.

What a stupid way to die.

Suddenly the cows parted, and I was free again, gasping.

"Rabi! Use the other fence!" Joe and Miguel shouted. They were pointing along the fence to a corner of the corral.

Still gasping, I started to run, dodging and weaving between the cows, trying not to slip in manure and get trampled. Just on the other side of the fence, the zombie kept pace, growling and looking for a way through to me. A cow blocked my way. I slid under it like I was stealing home, plowing through manure and missing hooves by inches. Came out on its far side and scrambled to my feet.

"Come on, Rabi!"

Ahead of me, Miguel and Joe were waving from the corral's corner. The perpendicular fence was lined with some kind of automated feed-trough system. If I could make it there, I was pretty sure I'd be able to climb back on the fences and also stay out of reach of the growling zombie beside me. I put my head down and ran.

A new surge of cows came surging toward me. A tidal wave of thousand-pound animals, galloping and mooing.

I put on a burst of speed. I didn't have time to climb the fence. I'd be crushed by the cows before I got up and over the troughs.

Instead, I dove.

I tumbled underneath the feed troughs just before the cows rammed up against them. Wood fencing crackled and snapped. The cows mooed hysterically and the metal troughs screeched and bent above my head. From where I crouched down in the muck, all I could see was trampling legs and hooves. For the first time in my life I was glad I was small. If I hadn't been able to duck under the feed troughs and take shelter—

A bony hand grabbed my ankle.

"Yow!" Jack-in-the-box zombie again. It'd managed to shove an arm through the fence and grab me. I tried to kick it away, but it was latched on like a pit bull.

"Brrrrrrrrains!" the zombie growled as it dragged me toward its mouth.

Suddenly a cow stepped on the zombie's arm. Bone cracked. I yanked my leg away hard, but the zombie didn't let go. Instead, the arm tore apart right where the cow had stamped on it. The whole thing came free, but with the zombie's hand still latched to my ankle.

The zombie howled at its lost hand and jerked back to its side of the fence, growling and shaking its head like a rabid dog. I tucked myself deeper under the feed troughs as I tried to pry the fingers of the severed hand off my ankle. The fingers fought me, but I finally tore the hand free and flung it out into the middle of the corral.

Now one-armed, my jack-in-the-box zombie friend was still trying to grab for me, but with only one remaining hand, I figured it wasn't as dangerous. I waited for a gap in the stampeding cows. . . .

There!

I popped out from under the feed troughs and hauled myself up and over the metal rim, to kneel in the ground corn feed, gasping for breath.

Miguel and Joe were waving for me. "Come on!"

But something wedged in the trough caught my eye. A Milrow smiling cow logo . . .

Without thinking, I reached into the trough and pulled it out of the feed. It was a Milrow ID badge with Mr. Cocoran's face on it. And another thing, shiny. *What the—?*

I shoved my hand deeper into the feed and yanked

out...a big plastic sack with a bunch of injection needles in it.

Weird, I thought, but I didn't have time to puzzle about it because the pop-up zombie had finally figured out that all it needed to do to get me was climb the fence. And even one-armed, it was managing it.

"*Gaahahaghghag,*" it growled as it hauled itself up.

"What are you doing, Rabi? He's coming!" Miguel and Joe shouted.

Clutching the badge and the bag, I clambered up the fence, barely beating the zombie to the top. It tried to bite me as I heaved myself up, but now I had the advantage. I kicked it in the head, and it plunged back into the zombie cow corral with a shriek.

Joe and Miguel cheered. I teetered over to them, and we quickly balance-beamed our way out of the corrals, leaving the shrieking zombie far behind. At last, we all jumped down beside the sewage lagoons.

Safe.

"I thought you were dead," Miguel said, grabbing me.

Joe started to hug me, then pulled back. "Dude. You're a mess."

"Did you get it on video?" I panted. "Did you get it? Do you still have the phone?"

"What phone?" Joe asked. But when he saw my

203

panicked face, he laughed. "Quit worrying. I got the whole thing."

"What's that you found?" Miguel asked me.

"Mr. Cocoran's Milrow badge. And a bunch of needles. I don't know what they are."

I wiped the dirty badge off on my filthy jeans and studied the picture. Mr. Cocoran looked a lot better in his company photo than he had the last time we saw him. His title was on the badge.

"'SuperGrow technician,'" I read. "What's that?"

"Remember my uncle said something about them giving the cows some kind of special growth drugs? To make them fatter."

We studied the syringes. Each one was labeled, too. "Milrow Bovine Growth Supplement, ten percent. Varacal, five percent. Torox, eight percent. Penicillin, twelve percent. NutriProtea, twenty percent…" The list went on. "Dude, what is all this stuff?"

"All the junk they put in the cows, I think. You know, to SuperGrow them."

"They're already plenty big for me," I said.

"Not for Milrow. Every pound of meat on the hoof means more cash for them," Miguel said.

I was trying to figure it out. Was there a connection here? "So, Mr. Cocoran was one of the guys who injected the cows with all these weird ingredients? He'd give them these drugs...." It didn't make sense. "So did he make the zombies?"

"Maybe he just got ambushed by one that was already out there," Joe said. "You got to admit, if you were going to write an origin story for evil, these feedlots would do the trick. Evil monsters always come from nasty places like nuclear waste dumps and swamps. Check this place out. I mean, seriously. It's perfect."

We looked out at the seething masses of cows. Even the nonzombie ones were disgusting. The ground was covered with waste, and so were the cows, and there was nothing but reeking smells and flies and rot. Seven states' worth of beef, all penned together, acre after acre, festering...

I could imagine it, all right. Maybe one weird cow had been out here, getting more messed up and crazy from eating nasty stuff, mutating in these corrals. Or maybe it had gotten infected with some kind of twisted bacteria that lived in the manure gunk. Or maybe there'd been untested chemicals in Cocoran's syringes that had made the cows go bad. Or maybe it was all those things, mixed together.

It was so sick and nasty in the feedlots that you could imagine a thousand different things going wrong.

Whatever had caused it, Mr. Cocoran had paid the price.

"Uh-oh," Joe said, grabbing both of us. "Looks like we've got company."

A bunch of guys in gray jumpsuits like the ones we'd seen at the baseball field were coming from the direction of the meatpacking plant. You could see their heads above the fence lines as they moved down lanes between some of the corrals.

We ducked down.

"Do you think they saw us?"

"Be hard to miss us, the way we were all up on top of the corrals like that."

But they weren't coming toward the sewage lagoon, where we were hiding. They were headed somewhere else. I peeked up over the fence, craning my neck to see where they were headed. "What are they up to?"

"Who cares? Let's get out of here," Miguel said. "We got your evidence. Let's go."

"I want to see what they're doing. These are the same guys as the ones who grabbed that cow off the baseball field."

"The cleanup squad."

"Yeah."

We watched the bobbing heads of the cleanup squad

as they made their way through the corrals. When they got to the zombie cows, they started shouting. And then there was a crackling, zapping sound, followed by squealing.

The zombie cows started flowing out of their corral. "I think they opened a gate," Joe whispered.

"They're letting them run free?" I asked. "That's crazy!"

Throwing away caution, I climbed higher on the fence, trying to get a better view of what was happening across the feedlots.

A stream of zombie cows were being herded toward...

"Uh-oh."

"What?" Joe popped up, too, followed by Miguel.

The guys in the gray suits were zapping the zombie cows with cattle prods. The cows moved faster and faster, running like a frothing river, all of them mooing and screaming and biting one another. All of them stamped-ing toward these huge doors in the side of the Milrow meatpacking plant.

Over the doors, a faded sign was posted.

BEEF INTAKE

CHAPTER 28

"So they're really going to make zombie burgers?" Joe asked.

"They can't be," I said. "That would be insane."

"Don't forget who we're dealing with. These guys don't care about anything," Miguel said. "They deal with bad meat all the time. They'll just spray it with some ammonia and send it out like it's the freshest stuff in the world."

"You still got space on your phone?" I asked Joe.

"Sure."

"Good. We're going in, then."

Miguel shook his head. "The game's over, Rabi. We should just go back and give this to the police or something."

"You think they'll believe us?" I asked. "All we've got are pictures of some crazy cows."

"We got the zombie," Miguel said.

Joe shook his head. "No, we don't. You think I could film and dance on a fence at the same time?" He opened his phone and showed us the footage. The cows looked crazy, sure, but it all looked pretty low-res, and even Miguel had to admit it didn't do the job.

"We need to see what they're doing," I said. "Then we can report it. We need real proof. Something people can't say we faked for YouTube."

"Like what?" Miguel said. "You want to try to bust out a zombie cow and drag it back to town?"

"I want to go into that meatpacking plant, and I want to see what they're doing in there."

"And you want me to help."

Joe said, "It's a zombie uprising, man. If we don't work together, we're all toast. Pretty soon, zombies'll be like lice. Everywhere. You know you want to see that."

Miguel gave him a dirty look.

"Come on, Miguel," I said. "Don't give me that whole *Zombies won't cross the border* thing. This is all of us. We're all in this. Whatever Milrow's doing is going to affect everyone, sooner or later."

"I know I'm going to regret this," Miguel said, but he

went along as we hacked our way back through the corn and over to the Milrow Meat Solutions main entrance. We flopped down in the cornfields a hundred feet from the doors.

"There it is."

"You still got the key?" I asked.

"Yeah, but there's a ton of people around right now. As soon as they see a couple of kids, they'll kick us out."

"Should we wait until dark?"

"You want to be out here in the dark?" Joe asked.

"I thought you *loooved* all this zombie cow action."

"Not at night! I want to at least be able to see which direction they're coming from. And that one zombie's still roaming around."

"We need to get in during the right work hours," Miguel said. "Otherwise my uncle's key definitely won't work. These keys are set to only open doors during your shifts."

"Can you describe what the place looks like, inside?" I asked. "You think there's some place we can hide?"

Miguel shrugged. "Maybe one of the bathrooms. They got these bathrooms and changing rooms for all the workers, for washing off all the blood and everything, and they're pretty close to the doors. Nobody's in there when a shift is happening because everyone's trying to keep up the pace on the lines. Workers can't slow down or they get fired."

We needed to figure out some way to hang out inside and wait until things got quieter. "Okay," I said. "I've got an idea. We need a pen and paper and some tape, though. We need someone to go back to town."

"If we keep riding around on our bikes, I'm going to get picked up, for sure," Miguel said.

I looked at Joe. "You do it."

"Why me?"

"Because you look like an American."

"How come you're always telling me about how you're an American, too, and now I got to do all the work?" Joe groused.

"That's not what it's about," I said. "If they see Miguel, they'll grab him. Especially after that baseball bat stunt with his neighbor. If they see me, I'm connected to him on account of the last time the police hauled me in. But if they see you?

"Think about it like comic books. You're the invisible one. You come and go like the wind. No one even notices you. You're just part of town. Like the signs and the corn and the cows. Nothing to look at; move along, folks."

Joe started looking more excited. "I come and go like the wind. Invisible."

"You got it. It's your superpower. Now, you want to use your powers of invisibility for good? Or are you going to work for the bad guys?" I nodded over at the Milrow building.

"Okay, I'll do it."

And he was off. Just like that. *Whoosh*. Like the wind. Miguel was looking at me.

"What?" I asked.

"That was creepy," he said.

"What was?"

"The way you got inside Joe's head. One second he didn't want to do any work, the next second he thinks he's one of his comic book heroes, and he's riding all the way back to town."

I thought about it. "We all want to be important. I guess you just have to find some way to help people see why they are."

"I would have just yelled at him and told him to stop being a dumbwad."

"That wouldn't work with Joe. That's what his dad does. It just messes with him more. This way is better. Everyone wants to be a hero, right?"

"Not me. I just want to get the heck out of this place."

"No, you don't. Not really."

Miguel glared at me. "Yeah. I do. So leave me alone, all right?"

I shut up. We sat in the corn and waited, listening to the mooing of the cows in the feedlots, accompanied by other, stranger sounds that might have been cows screaming as they bit one another.

Miguel just stared into space, waiting.

I was getting more worried about him. No family. No future. It would make anyone crazy.

Miguel was wrong, I decided.

He might not want to be a hero, but it was starting to look like he needed to be one.

CHAPTER 29

"What's been happening?" Joe asked as he returned and flopped down beside us.

"Nothing," Miguel said. "Just them cows doing their zombie screaming thing."

"I got the paper and the tape. I got some flashlights, too."

"Where'd you get these?"

"Took 'em from my dad's toolbox." He tossed us some bottles of orange and blue rehydrating drink and some candy bars. "I brought provisions, too."

"Good thinking!"

I took the paper and pen from Joe and wrote some block letters on the paper as Miguel stared at the meatpacking plant.

"What are you doing?" Joe asked.

"Don't worry about it." I got some of the tape out, too. "Ready?"

Miguel flashed the key card and grabbed his baseball bat. "Born ready."

"Let's go."

We headed through the parking lot toward the workers' entrance. "You sure about this?" Joe asked, scanning the lot. "Shouldn't we be sneaky?"

"If we look sneaky, when they see us, they'll think we're sneaky," I said. "Act like you belong."

"We don't belong in a meatpacking plant!" Joe said.

"We do now. If someone stops us, we say we were playing ball and I fell down in the muck, and now we're looking for someplace to clean me up."

Joe held his nose. "Well, that's believable, at least."

We reached the door and Miguel swiped the key card through the door's reader. Nothing happened. My heart stopped.

Miguel slid the card again, slower. The light glowed green. I almost wanted to laugh. They might have gotten rid of the workers, but they hadn't gotten rid of the keys yet.

Miguel pulled the door open. "Gentlemen," he said, and waved us through. "Milrow Meat Solutions would like to welcome you to its state-of-the-art protein-processing facility."

Inside, Miguel walked down the hall like he owned it, and we followed. I wished I had that kind of swagger. A kid with a baseball bat, not afraid of anything. He turned and walked straight into the locker rooms.

We heard a voice. "What are you doing here, kid?"

Joe and I froze. *Busted.*

No one was supposed to be in the changing rooms. I half expected Miguel to just whack the guy with his bat, given the weird mood he was in.

Instead, we heard him say, "Janitor, *sí*?" and then a whole stream of Spanish that I didn't catch.

"You speak English?" the grown-up voice asked.

Miguel said, "Mop, *sí*? Mop, mop, *sí*?"

"Oh," the man's voice said, sounding uncertain as Miguel unleashed another stream of Spanish. "Uh. All that stuff is over here."

Their voices headed away from us. I motioned to Joe, and the two of us ducked into the changing rooms. At the far end, there was a row of toilet stalls, and on the last door, I taped the sign I'd made earlier.

OUT OF ORDER

"Get in there," I said.

"This isn't going to work," Joe said.

"We'll see. Climb up on the toilet. Don't let your feet show underneath."

We ducked inside and balanced inside the stall. I wondered what was happening with Miguel. I hoped he was okay.

"Dude, you smell," Joe said.

"Shut up!" I whispered.

Footsteps were echoing in the changing rooms. We both hunkered down. Someone rapped on the door.

"Open up," Miguel said. "I got a better plan."

When we opened the door, Miguel was standing there in a janitor's jumpsuit and holding a mop.

"Where'd you get all that?"

Miguel smirked. "Talk Spanish and these jerks all think you're supposed to have a mop in your hand." He waved us out. "Come on. I got a real place to hide." He wrinkled his nose at me. "And, dude, you got to get out of those clothes. Hurry, before some other manager comes down here. Shift change shouldn't happen for a little while, still."

It turned out there was a whole room with mops and brooms and tons of cleaning supplies. Miguel dumped

Joe in the closet and me in the shower, while he stood outside in his janitor uniform with a yellow bucket full of mop water. When I was clean, he tossed me another uniform that he'd found and crammed me into the closet with Joe.

"Stay put," he said.

"Wait! Where are you going?" I asked.

"I'm going to use my superpower of invisibility," Miguel smirked. "I'm going to come and go like the wind."

CHAPTER 30

By the time Miguel came back, Joe and I were dead bored. It felt like it had been hours.

"Where've you been?"

"All over," Miguel said. "They're just letting out the shift. We're going to have to get out of here fast, as soon they let out. After that, they got a bunch of janitors who all come in."

"How do you know?"

"The guy told me I was early."

"Should we all be janitors?" Joe asked.

"None of us can be, when the real janitors get here."

"They're going to want our suits back," Miguel agreed.

"So, what are we trying to find?" Joe asked.

"Something that the cops will actually care about," I

said. "Something Milrow's cleanup squad can't just scoop up and hide. And something that can't be denied by anyone."

We slipped out. The halls were dim with all the lights out, but we had flashlights. We tiptoed through the building.

"It's here," Miguel said, standing in front of some steel doors.

"What is?"

He didn't answer, just swung the doors open. We stood in a cavernous factory room tangled with conveyors and equipment: Meat hooks dangled from chains overhead, conveyor belts went every which way, and massive boxy machines that might have been grinders or other things—but I couldn't tell—were everywhere. The place was so big you couldn't even see the far side of it.

We eased into the space. It was scary, with all the chains and hooks hanging down from their conveyors.

"What are we looking for?" Joe asked.

"Something that looks zombie," I said. "Anything."

The concrete floors all glistened with water and blood, and everything gleamed. It was chilly, and it had the scent of a meat locker. It was like smelling life gone cold. Our breath steamed in front of us.

"What about the cows?" Joe asked. "Where did they go?"

Miguel waved toward the far side of the huge factory floor. "A bunch of them are in the next room over, in a huge pen. The cows get herded one by one up a ramp that leads into here—"

Suddenly there was a rattling sound. "Hide!"

We ducked behind the conveyor lines. Footsteps echoed, along with voices calling out to one another.

"I thought they were all supposed to be gone!" I whispered.

"Another shift?" Joe asked.

"No," Miguel said. "It's only supposed to be cleaning crews. The guy I talked to said they were going to be cleaning the whole plant, so the night shift wasn't going to run. Just cleaning."

Lights buzzed and flickered on. Workers in white full-body jumpsuits streamed in. Joe found a spot under some of the machinery. "Hide here!"

We just barely squeezed under.

"Don't let your feet stick out!" Miguel whispered. "They'll see us for sure."

It was tight, but we all fit. From our hiding place, we watched as more and more workers came in.

"Who do those guys remind you of?" I asked.

"Cleanup squad," Joe said grimly.

"Yeah. None of these are regular workers," Miguel said. "Not with those clothes covering their whole bodies like that. And they don't have aprons like my uncle and aunt used. These have got to be some other kind of Milrow people."

The conveyor lines started up. A door rattled and suddenly we could hear cows, screaming. More workers came in with huge knives and chain saw–like machines. They fired them up as the line started moving.

The first cow appeared. It had a huge hole in its head, but that didn't seem to bother the cow at all. A bunch of hooks snagged it and swept it off the ground as it struggled.

"MOOOOoooooooo!"

The workers went after it with knives and saws. The cow tried to bite them, but they were fast. Cutting and chopping, peeling away the skin. The head came off, the belly opened up, the guts went down a drain. The cow's head fell to the floor.

"MOOOOOOooooooooo," it said. Its hooked body was still jerking around even without its head.

"Zombie cow for sure," Joe said, as if we needed him

to tell us. The cow was still alive, even though it was completely dead.

One of the workers got kicked by the dead cow, but he got right up and chopped the carcass in half. Then water sprayed it and the next worker whacked off the legs. The carcass whizzed along, carried by the hooks, with more workers slicing cuts of meat from the body, even as it kept wriggling.

The zombie cow became smaller and smaller, and less and less like a cow, as each worker took a whack at it. Pieces and parts were slashed and sliced away, and dropped onto conveyor belts that whisked the meat this way and that through the processing plant, heading for who knew where.

Another cow entered the production line, and the cleanup squad went after that one, too.

"MOOooooooo!"

Slice! Hack! Chop!

ZZzZzz-ZZZZzzzzz-ZZZZZZ went the chain saws.

Another cow whacked into little red pieces.

More of the line was gearing up. It was crazy loud in the factory now, like we were in the belly of a clanging monster. Ground-up meat oozed out of delivery tubes, and newly cut steaks whipped down conveyor lines, shrink-wrapped in plastic.

More and more cows were being herded in through the doors, and every single one of them was mooing, even after it was chopped up and dead. The cow heads that had been discarded lay in a huge pile, snapping at one another and at any workers who walked past them.

Pound after pound of red hamburger poured out of the machines around us, blobs of beef that dropped onto Styrofoam plates and then went through shrink-wrapping machines so that they came out on the other side looking shiny and fresh, with Milrow stickers on the plastic.

Labels sped past us:

FARMERS FEAST 100% ALL-NATURAL GROUND BEEF.

FOREST GLEN ACRES, PURE GROUND BEEF.

HIGH PLAINS RANCHES, USDA NATURAL GROUND BEEF.

MILROW MEATS. TOP-QUALITY BEEF FROM OUR FAMILY RANCHES TO YOUR FAMILY TABLE.

Joe had his cell phone out and he was snapping pictures, looking sick. "I think I'm a vegetarian."

Miguel gave him an annoyed glance. "Where did you think all your meat came from? You think it just *bamf*ed into the supermarket like Nightcrawler?"

I had to agree with Joe, though. It was brutal and nasty. None of the workers seemed to be worried about what they were doing at all. They were just being super-efficient. Even if there hadn't been zombie cow heads lying on the ground, mooing and rolling their eyes and snapping their teeth, the whole setup didn't feel good to watch.

I mean, I went out with my dad once to a farm, where we bought a sheep for mutton, and we saw the farmer kill the sheep. He stuck his knife into the sheep's throat, and we watched him kill it, and it was uncomfortable, because you could see that something was dying so you could eat it . . . but killing a sheep up close and personal wasn't like this. The sheep bled and got chopped up, and Dad and I ate it, sure, but this Milrow factory was something else. Cow after cow coming into the plant and getting ripped to pieces. High-speed chopping ripping tearing shrink-wrapping. I wondered what kind of people could create a factory like this, all for tearing animals apart as fast as possible. It scared me.

"They're turning all the zombie cows into food for people," I said. "I can't believe it. They're insane."

It was all zombie cows. Not a single real cow in the whole bunch.

"So this is what ground zero for the zombie apocalypse looks like." Joe snapped more pics. "I sort of thought it would be a military science lab somewhere."

"We've got to stop this," I said. "We can't let them do this."

"There's a STOP button on the line," Joe said.

Miguel whacked him upside the head. "Not just now, idiot. We got to report it. Make sure *all* this gets stopped."

"We need something they can't sweep under the table," I said. "Something cops can't ignore."

"Real zombie proof," Joe murmured.

"Something that you just couldn't make up," Miguel said.

"MOOOOOOOOOoooooooooooo!" moaned the cow heads, lying in a giant pile at the beginning of the meat-packing line. "MOOOOooooooooooooooooooo!"

We all looked at each other.

A mooing zombie cow head?

Yeah. That would probably do the trick.

CHAPTER 31

"Once we grab one, we've got to be ready to run," Joe said. "They'll be all over us."

"What do you think, Rabi?" Miguel asked. "You got some kind of superstrategy for this?"

I looked over the line, trying to figure out the best way. "If we grab the head, they're going to see us and we'll never outrun them on our bikes." A new idea hit me. "You still got the keys to your uncle's truck?"

Miguel looked puzzled, then felt his pockets, "I don't . . ." His eyes widened. "Yeah. Right here."

"You think you can drive us out of here?" I asked. "Without crashing?"

Miguel thought about it. "Sure. As long as I don't have to reverse."

"Are we leaving our bikes?" Joe asked.

"Forget the bikes," I said. "We're trading up."

"This is nuts," Joe said. "Miguel could get busted driving illegally."

Miguel laughed. "You're going to worry about me driving without a license? I'm not even licensed to *walk* in America. Everything I do here is illegal. I'll totally drive us out of here."

"As long as we get ourselves a zombie cow head, nothing else will matter," I said. "If the cops see one of those monsters, they're going to forget all about who's driving what or where someone was born."

"Just be careful not to get bit," Miguel said.

"We got gloves or something?"

"Worker gloves. Sure." Miguel stealthed off as I continued to look over the line.

When Miguel came back with gloves, I said, "Here's what we do. Miguel goes and gets the truck running. Joe, you're getting the head."

"Sweeeeeet." Joe paused, then asked, "So, what are you doing?"

I sighed. "I'm the bait. Just like always."

"Will you at least grab my bat?" Joe asked Miguel.

"Don't worry. I'll dump everything in the truck," Miguel said.

We all got set. I gave Miguel a four hundred count to get out to the truck and get it loaded.

"You set?" I asked Joe.

Joe grinned. "Me? I'm born ready. You think Miguel is?"

I wasn't, but I didn't want to hang out in the factory any longer. The longer we waited, the bigger the chance that we'd get caught. "He'd better be," I said. "Let's do it."

Joe started sneaking around the side of the line, ducking and keeping to the shadows, pausing behind machinery, sliding under conveyors. Waiting until workers' backs were turned before bolting from one hiding place to the next. He was good at it.

More cows were dragged in, hooked up, and gutted. The pile of mooing cow heads grew. More meat whipped past me in little plastic packages.

Where was it all going?

I spared a quick glance at Joe and his sneaky progress around the production lines. He was tucked into deep shadow between a couple of big metal grinders. You could barely make him out.

More burger shot past me on conveyors, with no sign of where it was all going. Were they going to bury it? Were they storing it?

I squeezed out of my hiding place and snuck down the line, trying to convince myself that I wasn't messing

229

up the plan. Anyway, I just needed to create a distraction. The farther away I was from Joe when I raised a holler, the better.

The line workers didn't notice a thing. It was lucky that they were all covered head to toe in protective gear, and the line was going so fast. No wonder Miguel's family had always been tired when they came home from working at Milrow: the whole plant was running on fast-forward, like some kind of superfast video game that never gave you a chance to breathe before the next cow came whipping down the line. The workers had to chop it up before the next one came crashing down on them. They had to stay totally focused and didn't have time to do anything at all except work work work.

At least it made it easy for me to sneak behind them and run down the line to where the meat was disappearing into the storage areas.

I peered into the freezer room and sucked in my breath.

When I'd seen the labels, I should have known. A half-dozen big refrigerated trucks were backed up to the loading docks, and workers were shoveling meat into the trucks as fast as it came off the production line. As each truck filled, another took its place.

I remembered Miguel's uncle telling us that meat from Milrow was delivered to seven states.

This was the beginning of the real honest-to-God zombie apocalypse. Truck after truck carrying zombified meat to supermarkets and fast-food restaurants all across America's heartland. Ground zero for the end of the world, just like Joe had been saying.

If Americans eat x *pounds of beef each week, and it takes* m *cows to make enough, and if Milrow feeds seven states with a population of* p…

It added up to a lot of zombies.

Where were all the inspectors? Why wasn't anyone catching this? How could Milrow get away with it?

A shout echoed from the meatpacking room. All of a sudden the line stopped running. More people started shouting, and then I could hear Joe hooting and hollering. All the loading workers ran toward the commotion.

I caught a glimpse of Joe dashing down a conveyor belt, laughing like a maniac. He held a snapping cow head high, and it let out a crazed "MOOOOOoooo!" as Joe dodged the clumsy grabs of suited-up workers.

I couldn't believe it. He hadn't even waited for my signal. He'd just gone for it. Typical Joe. And now he was going to get snagged, unless—

"I got one, too!" I shouted at them. "Look at me! I got one, too, and you didn't even see it!" They all turned and stared at me. I saw Joe duck through beginning of the line, through the hole where the cows had all been coming in, and then he was gone.

Some workers were scrambling after Joe, but others started for me. I bolted back into the shipping room.

Right in front of me, one of the trucks was idling.

I realized what I had to do.

It wouldn't do any good to have zombie proof if we didn't know where they were taking all this meat. I dove into the truck and buried myself under cold blocks of meat.

I heard men shouting, "Where'd he go? Where is he? You see him, Pete?"

And then someone else said, "Get everything cleaned up and get these trucks out of here! I don't want anything for an inspector to see if those kids call USDA!"

One of the workers laughed at that. "When does USDA ever see anything? I've got a blind aunt who sees better than USDA." And then the doors rattled closed and darkness swallowed me.

It was cold.

Really cold.

All I had on were thin Milrow janitor clothes.

The truck started to drive and I got colder and colder. My teeth started to chatter. I tried to get up and keep moving, but I couldn't stand straight because the truck

232

kept speeding up and slowing down and turning corners. I squatted down in a corner, trying to stay away from the freezing walls, wrapping my arms around myself in the darkness.

It was insanely cold. Too cold. I realized I was going to die. Someone was going find me here, huddled up—a frozen Rabi Popsicle surrounded by piles of zombie meat.

What a stupid way to die.

I hadn't stopped the zombie apocalypse, and I hadn't saved anyone. Nothing I'd done had mattered.

I might have felt bad about that, but I was getting too cold to feel much about anything one way or the other.

By the time the zombies got done with America, I was going to be long gone.

It got colder and colder.

And colder.

colder

co—

...

CHAPTER 32

The door to the meat truck rolled up.

The light was so bright I couldn't see.

"Get him out of there!"

Who was that?

Shadows grabbed me and dragged me out of the truck. Humid air blasted over me. Warm air. Someone was holding me up, but when they let me go, I just fell over. I hit the pavement with a *thud*.

A blanket dropped on me. "Get under it."

Miguel?

"Get under it?"

That was Joe.

"He's frozen. He doesn't have any heat inside him anymore. We got to warm him up."

"His skin is like ice."

Popsicle, I wanted to say, but I couldn't make my jaw work. *Rabi Popsicle.* They climbed under the blanket with me and hugged me.

"Next time you decide to be a hero, maybe you should think a little before you do it," Miguel said.

"Yeah, man," Joe said. "Leave the crazy stuff to me."

They were chafing my arms and legs. My limbs were tingling, getting their feeling back. I started to shiver.

"He's getting worse!" Joe said.

"No," Miguel said. "He's getting better. His body's remembering that it's cold. Now it's trying to warm up. Shivering is how he warms up."

I sat up and pushed them off. Miguel looked me over. "You okay?"

"Y-ye-yeah," I said. "I'm ff-f-f-f—fine."

"He's alive, ladies and gentlemen," Joe said. "The first ever Neanderthal to be pulled out of a glacier."

My head hurt. I was still freezing. I tried to get up and stumbled and sat down again. I couldn't stop shivering. Miguel grabbed me and said, "Slow down, boy hero."

"Q-q-quit calling me th-that."

"Then quit doing stupid stuff. If you're gonna be some kind of big strategy guy, then you got to think at least more than one step ahead. What the heck were you thinking?"

"I d-d-didn't w-want to let the t-t-truck get away. D-d-d-didn't want to lose the mmmm-m-meat." I looked around. "W-where are we? H-h-how'd you find me? I thought I was a g-goner."

Joe grinned. "Thank Miguel. He saw you jump in."

"Dumbest thing I ever saw," Miguel said. "You know how many trucks they put out on the road? We almost lost you twice, trying to follow yours in the dark. If Joe didn't get the license plate, you'd have been dead for sure. Most of them turned one way, but Joe noticed yours wasn't there anymore, so we tracked back and found it."

"Wh-where are we?"

"The Hy-Vee."

"The supermarket? Here in Delbe?"

"We think they're going to put the meat into the store."

Another shiver overtook me. "They c-c-can't!"

"Yeah. We're trying to figure out what to do."

"Where's the driver?"

Joe looked embarrassed. "I used the cow on him."

"You did *what*?"

"He noticed we were following him and he got out

and came after us. He looked really mad, and then he tried to grab us. So I threw the cow at him."

"And it bit him?"

"Yeah. Now he's over in those weeds. We tied him up."

"You can't just go making zombies!"

"He had a tire iron! He was going to hit us!"

I shook my head. "I can't leave you guys for a s-s-second."

"Save it, Popsicle boy," Miguel said. "Without us, you'd be dead by now."

"Making more zombies doesn't stop the zombie apocalypse," I said.

"Getting our heads bashed in by some grown-up doesn't stop it, either," Miguel said. "Joe might be crazy, but that guy was going to kill us."

"Okay," I said. "You're right. I'm sorry. Thanks for saving me." I paused. "So, what are we going to do about the meat?"

"We can burn it," Joe suggested.

"Like with a bonfire?"

Joe grinned. "Well...kind of."

CHAPTER 33

The truck blew up.

I expected it to be more spectacular, but it turned out that if we soaked our shirts in gas from the can Miguel used for his mower, and then lit them with the lighter, they went up pretty good.

The fire ran from shirt to shirt, igniting each one in the line. *Whump whump whump!* Fast. And then flaming right up a knotted shirt and into the gas tank of the truck. We ducked behind the Hy-Vee.

Bam! Up went the truck. No more meat.

We came out and watched it burn. Orange and yellow flames roiled. Oily smoke billowed up into the night sky, blotting out stars and moon. The heat made my face and body warm. I'd never blown up a truck before.

"It's not as good as in the movies," Joe groused. "Comic books and movies get it all wrong."

"As long as it's getting rid of the meat," I said, "it's fine. Now let's get out of here."

"But it was supposed to be really big!" Joe complained. "I wanted, like, a mushroom cloud or something."

"It's doing the job," Miguel said. "Now get in. We're going to be in serious trouble if anyone catches us here." He opened the door of his uncle's pickup truck.

"There's no one around here this late," Joe said, still watching the meat truck burn.

"Where's the cow?" I asked.

A mooing came from the back of the pickup, answering the question. I walked over and looked into the truck bed. There it was, baring its teeth, like it wanted to bounce up and start chewing on me.

"I was trying to come up with names for it," Joe said.

"You what?"

"At first, I was thinking Bessie, but I think it's a boy."

"A steer," Miguel corrected.

"Whatever. Its name is Bart."

"Bart?"

"Bart the Zombie Cow." Joe reached out to pat it on the top of its head. It snapped and he jerked his hand back.

"Don't touch it!" Miguel and I both shouted.

Joe looked at us like we were babies. "I'm not afraid of it. I'm the one who grabbed it in the first place. Sheesh. It's not like he's got legs or something. Not like he can jump." He climbed into the truck and looked ahead. "So, are we going, or what?"

Bart the Zombie Cow. Miguel and I stared at it. Or him. Or Bart. Or whatever.

The head glared at us and bared its teeth again. "Mooooooooooo."

If there was any better proof that something wasn't right at Milrow Meat Solutions, I couldn't think of it. If the cops didn't believe this, they wouldn't believe anything.

"You ready to finish this?" Miguel asked.

"More than ready."

We climbed in and Miguel peeled out of the parking lot, leaving the burning Milrow meat truck flickering in our rearview mirror.

We headed down Grand Avenue toward the police station. The five lights on the main drag were all green, and we rolled right through, like the universe was telling us that all was good, and we were on the road to salvation.

We pulled into the police station and parked.

"Well, here we are," Miguel said.

"It's awful dark," Joe said.

He was right. I squinted at the place. There weren't any lights on at all. "What time is it?" I asked.

"Must be after midnight."

"Do they close?"

"Beats me. I never tried to visit a police station in the middle of the night."

We got out and went over to the doors. Joe rattled them, but they were locked. A moaning broke the silence. We all knew instantly what that meant.

"Get the bats!"

We dashed back to the truck and grabbed our sluggers. The moaning came again.

"Who's there?" I shouted, ready for a zombie to come bursting out of the bushes. Slowly, a shadow rose. We spread out, raising our bats.

"Whoa!" the shadow called. "Go easy!"

"Otis?" I asked. "Is that you?"

Sure enough, it was Otis Andrews, stepping out of the shadows, holding a baseball bat of his own.

"Get him!" Joe shouted, but Miguel grabbed Joe by the shirt and yanked him back.

"He isn't a zombie, dumbwad."

"We don't know that," Joe said.

"You zombied?" I asked Otis.

"Nah, man." He shrugged. "But only because you warned me."

Another moaning came from the shadows.

"So what's that sound?"

"Bart," Otis said.

"Bart's in the truck," Joe said.

I lowered my baseball bat. "He means Bart Lewis," I said. "Not your pet cow."

Otis led us over to where the moaning was coming from. He had Bart chained to a bike rack. Bart caught sight of us and reached out, straining to get hold of—

"BRAAAaaaaiinnnnsssss…"

"Man," Miguel said. "That's sad."

Otis nodded. "The really sad thing is that I think he's actually smarter this way."

"What happened?"

"You were right," Otis said. "He just turned on me. One second he was yelling about how he was going to kill that cow and how he was going to kill you guys and how he was going to kick some serious butt—next thing you know, he's stumbling around trying to bite anything that moves. If I hadn't been watching for it, he would've got me."

"How'd you tie him up?"

Otis flexed his muscles. "I'm bigger. And he's real clumsy now." He sighed. "But I don't know what to do with him. I don't want to take him back to his folks, 'cause I don't think they'd understand that it was an accident, and I don't want to get yelled at. And I really don't want anyone else to get bit, 'cause that don't seem right." He shrugged. "So I figured I'd bring him down here and maybe the cops could help me sort it out."

"They're gone," Joe said.

"Figured that out myself. I never really thought about it, but I guess police don't work nights unless they're city cops."

Bart the Zombie moaned.

Behind us, Bart the Zombie Cow answered.

It was creepy. Like they were talking to each other. Planning something. "He tied up good?" Miguel asked.

"Yeah."

"Leave him," Miguel said. "The cops will find him tomorrow."

"What if they get bit?"

We all looked at each other. "I got a Magic Marker in the truck," I said.

With Otis's help, we pinned Bart down and I used a Sharpie to write on his forehead.

ZOMBIE! BEWARE BITING!

If they couldn't read the warning, then there wasn't much else we could do. We all stood back.

"Good enough?"

"Yeah. That does the job."

As we were all separating, Otis said, "You coming to the baseball game tomorrow?"

We all looked at each other. We'd totally forgotten about the game.

"It's not canceled?" I asked.

"Nah. I got a call on the phone tree. It's still on. Sammy's dad is volunteering to coach."

"Sammy's dad, huh?" We all exchanged glances. "Sammy and his dad..."

Otis caught my tone, but he misunderstood what I was thinking. "He won't mess with you at the game."

Miguel said, "That kid's meaner than a snake. No telling what he'll do. Him or his dad."

"Yeah, well, I owe you," Otis said. "Nothing's happening to you at the game. As long as we're playing baseball, we're a team, and as long as we're a team, I'll keep Sammy on a leash. There won't be any trouble from him. Promise."

"Thanks, Otis," I said.

"No worries." He nodded at Bart. "Keep your eye out for zombies."

"You, too."

He disappeared into the darkness. A big old slugger, heading home. It was kind of cool to think of us all being on the same team. I wished I felt like that more. And then I wondered if it just took something bigger, like zombies, to make things clear. Otis was all right. Maybe he always had been.

"So, Sammy's dad is going to be at the game tomorrow," Miguel said.

"What a pain."

I mostly didn't want to have to deal with Sammy or his dad. And I definitely didn't care about the distraction of a baseball game when more important things were going on.

Joe mirrored my thoughts. "Is there even any point in going?"

"Hold on," Miguel said. "You know how Sammy's dad is always on TV, talking about how Milrow's a good neighbor, and provides jobs, and feeds people and all that stuff?"

"Yeah, so?"

"I was just thinking it might be kind of cool if we could stick it to the guy who got my family deported, you know? You know, really jam him up somehow, seeing as we know where he's going to be tomorrow, and what he's going to be doing…"

Behind us, Bart the Zombie Cow mooed again, low and hungry.

Miguel went on, "I was thinking it might be cool if Mr. Riggoni, senior executive of Milrow Meat Solutions, met our friend Bart the Zombie Cow on live TV."

CHAPTER 34

You could practically see the headlines:

ZOMBIE COW AND MILROW EXECUTIVE FACE OFF!
MILROW EMBARRASSED BY MAN-EATING COW HEAD!

It was too good to pass up, so we headed right back to my house to make a plan.

It took some phone calls and some Googling around to figure out what we needed to do and who we needed to call. We had to practice a script—and not crack up while we were doing it—and then we had to wait for morning work hours to start before we could make the call.

Amazingly, Joe was the only one who could make it all the way through our script. He deepened his voice and just went at it. It was impressive to see how good he was at faking being a grown-up.

"I did this once when I needed to call an 800 number to order off the TV," Joe explained. "I had to sound like my mom. Total pain to make my voice go like that."

And then the phone was ringing, and his voice went down a notch and he became someone else.

"Yes, this Sam Drexel, over at Milrow media relations. I'm just calling to let you know that our Delbe facility's senior executive, Mr. David Riggoni, will be stepping in to coach our local Little League team this afternoon, and he'd love to have a chance to talk about how wonderful our local youth are, and how Milrow has been supporting youth in…in…"

"Initiatives," I whispered urgently.

Joe waved me off, irritated. "Initiatives! We'd really like to encourage others in the community to come out and support sports and the positive impact it has on youth. These kids have been swinging hard all season, and we'd love to see them recognized, so Mr. Riggoni will be presenting them with a special surprise that we think will be newsworthy—and is better seen on television, rather than in print. It'll be a fantastic news opportunity for your station, and we're letting you know, exclusively."

Joe had gone off script. I slapped his knee, but he kept going, grinning now. "Well, I'll just say, the kids will never forget this particular surprise. Of course, I'm not at liberty to speak about it until the unveiling, but it won't be a waste of your time to cover the event. A real scoop. I've worked here for a long time, and I have to say, I've never seen anything quite like it. I guarantee good viewing. In fact, I'd stake my job on it."

I smacked Joe's knee again, but he just kept going, buttering up whoever was on the other end.

"That's right. At the Delbe Middle School baseball diamond. One PM. We'll look forward to seeing you there."

The person on the other end said something. Joe covered the mouthpiece. "He wants to know if we've got a press pack?"

We both shrugged.

Joe said, "At the game. We'll have a bunch of them." He hung up fast.

"You went off the script!" I said.

"I was making it better."

"Do you think they'll come?" Miguel asked. "Did you convince them?"

"Who knows? They kind of sounded bored. Like they'd heard all that stuff before. I don't think they really like 'media relations' guys very much. We should have given me a different title or something."

"Well, it's too late now. Anyway, we've got to get to the game."

Miguel and I put on our baseball gear, and then we realized we still needed to haul Bart the Zombie Cow, without getting bit.

"I can drive," Miguel suggested.

"Are we seriously going to drive the truck to the game?" I asked. "That's just asking for trouble."

"We got to hit my house first," Joe said. "I need to get the rest of my gear."

"Joe's house, and then the game, too? We're pushing our luck."

"It's better than hauling that cow head by hand," Miguel said. "You don't seriously want to sling Bart in a sack and bike him around, right?"

He was right: I didn't.

So we drove. Miguel stayed on the backstreets so we wouldn't run into the cops, but it felt different, riskier, to be driving around in broad daylight. We were going to get busted for sure. Even though Miguel was getting better at driving, there was no way we could keep testing our luck.

But we made it. We parked at the far side of the middle school's lot so fewer people would notice us getting out, and then we walked down to the dugout.

The other team was there already, hitting balls. I caught sight of Otis, and then Sammy.

"Seriously?" Miguel said, as Sammy came storming toward us.

"Nice shiners, dumbwads," Sammy said. "Back for more?"

Otis came up behind him. "Leave them alone," he said. "They're all right."

"You've got to be kidding." Sammy spat on the ground right in front of my feet.

As much as I would've loved to taunt Sammy, I didn't take the bait. I just pulled Joe and Miguel away before any of us did anything stupid. Starting a fight when grown-ups weren't around was one thing. Brawling in front of every family in town, along with the enemy team, was something else.

"Come on," I said. "We've got bigger fish to fry. Let's go warm up."

We went out and started throwing balls. Just easy catches, back and forth, limbering up. Miguel picked up a bat and started swinging it.

More parents and kids started arriving. Sammy's dad was walking around, looking kind of smug. Miguel studied him real hard.

I realized Miguel was standing less than thirty feet from the guy who'd gotten Miguel's entire family deported. The guy who got rid of Milrow workers who knew too much. I could see the gears whizzing in Miguel's head. Not a good sign. I went over and grabbed his shoulder.

"You're practically staring laser holes through Riggoni," I said.

"I can't help it. I hate that guy."

"Well, that's why we're doing this, right?"

"If the cameras show up."

"They'll show." *I hoped.* "Stay chill. The last thing we need is Riggoni calling ICE on you."

We got ourselves warmed up and the other team came out on the field. Joe tapped my shoulder. "Check it out."

Up on the hill, a TV crew had appeared. I nudged Miguel. "Score."

Miguel started smiling. We just had to get through the game, then get Mr. Riggoni in front of the cameras. Steer that sucker right in front of those cameras he liked so much. And then Joe would bring Bart the Zombie

Cow in for his star turn on broadcast TV. The head of Milrow Meats, with the head of its product.

I had to hand it to Miguel—it was genius.

But first we had to get through our game, and switching coaches wasn't going to do much for us. Mr. Cocoran might have been a terrible coach, but Sammy's dad was worse. He wanted Miguel first in the lineup, when he should have been cleanup. He had no idea what our signs were, so he started making up his own, and started trying to get us to memorize them, right then.

You could tell it was going to be a mess.

Finally, I just couldn't take it. I was sick of watching idiots act like they knew stuff, when they didn't. I was tired of watching everything go wrong and not doing anything about it. I raised my hand. Mr. Riggoni saw my hand waving, and at first he tried to ignore it, but I kept it up, and finally he gave up on talking about how three fingers on the shoulder was going to mean a sacrifice bunt.

"What do you want?"

"We might do better if we just changed our batting order."

"Say again?"

"Changing our signs isn't going to do a whole lot. But

if we change our batting order, we can do better," I said. "It's got to do with batting statistics. Miguel almost always gets at least a double, so if you get some other guys out who hit singles, then he gets two, maybe three people in, every time he comes up. He could have crazy RBIs, but we don't have him in the right place. And with Otis, he's a power hitter, so—"

"Sit down," Mr. Riggoni said.

"But—"

Sammy's dad looked at me like I was a bug. "I know you think you're some kind of math genius or something, Jones, but show some respect when you talk to me."

"I *am* showing respect," I said. "I'm just saying—"

"Sit down!"

I sat.

"You're such a dumbwad," Sammy said. "Don't tell my dad what to do."

But I thought some of the other guys on the team had been listening. Otis met my eye, and then just sort of shook his head, like he was saying, *Don't sweat it.*

The more I saw of Otis, the more I liked him. He was mean and tough, but he shot straight. If you were straight with him, he was straight with you. That simple. You could work with a guy like Otis.

Sammy, though? Or his dad?

They were just grudges and ego. There was no point talking to them. They weren't going to listen, anyway. I leaned back on the bench, watching as Mr. Riggoni set up an even worse batting order than Mr. Cocoran's. At least I'd tried.

The game started up and it went just as bad as I expected. Sammy's dad kept yelling at us when we missed a ball, and when we didn't (or did) try to steal a base, or when we didn't understand one of the new signals he'd made up. We struck out and we fouled out. We missed easy plays because Riggoni was shouting so much. It was embarrassing.

The innings came and went and the heat got worse. We all drank Gatorade and sweated and we lost and lost and lost.

I went out to bat, and once again, I was batting cleanup, with Alan and Sid on first and second. The chances of me singling were tiny, and the chances of my getting out were ridiculously high, so all that work of getting guys on base was going to be wasted. I just wasn't a hitter.

So, what? Bunt? Swing for the fences anyway and pray that Ganesha would hook me up with some kind of crazy line drive? I'd always loved the numbers of baseball, but the batting? It was never really my thing.

I stood out there in the hot sun, with the whole crowd watching me. People in bleachers. People sitting on blankets on the grass with bright umbrellas stuck in the ground. They were all watching. Even Officer Baby Face Boone was there to watch another round of Rabi humiliation.

Just get through the game.

The pitcher knew he could cream me. But maybe I could fake him out somehow. Make him give me a nice fastball that I could smack. I brought up my bat.

"Strike one!"

The pitch was so fast that I barely saw it. I started to get ready again, trying to remember what Miguel had been teaching me about being a baseball-killing machine…but something caught my eye. I paused, staring up at the crowds.

A truck. Right at the top of the rise. One of those snack vendor trucks with a side that opens up, and a kitchen inside it. And on the top, in big letters, it read:

MILROW MEATS, ALL-NATURAL QUALITY.

There was a long line of people outside it.

As I watched, the cook passed a burger out to one of the many, many, *many* hungry people who were lined up for lunch.

I didn't even see the next ball as it whizzed across the plate.

I was too busy watching people all over the hillside, as they chowed down on Milrow's all-natural quality zombie cow.

CHAPTER 35

I was out, and didn't care a bit.

Sammy passed me on the way to the plate. "Nice going, loser. You could at least swing at the ball, instead of staring off into space."

A few days ago, I would have been bothered. Now, I hardly even noticed.

I sat down on the bench, beside Joe and Miguel. "Um, guys?"

"Hmm?" Miguel was still glaring at Sammy's dad. "What?"

"What do you see up there?"

Miguel didn't turn. But Joe did. He did a double take. "That can't be good."

"I think the word you're looking for is *disaster*."

Miguel finally focused on us. "What's wrong?"

Joe was reaching under the bench and grabbing his bat. "I think we got ourselves a real-life, honest-to-God zombie apocalypse on our hands."

Miguel stared up at the crowds and the meat truck. "You know, people say Mexico's bad, but I really am starting to think my family were the lucky ones."

"Where's ICE when we need them, right?" Joe said. "I'd totally go for a deportation right about now."

"How many bats we got?" Miguel asked.

"Not enough." I leaned down the line. "Hey, Otis!"

He looked up.

"How long did it take Bart to turn into a zombie?"

"I don't know. About half an hour. Why?"

"You bring an extra bat?"

"No." He gave me a funny look. "Why?"

I jerked my thumb toward the stands. "You see the meat they're serving up there? All that cow?" I pointed up at the vendor truck on the hillside. "There's a good chance I'm going to need a good, hard slugger on my team. Real. Soon."

Otis stared up at the meat truck. "What's wrong with the meat...?" He trailed off. I could see his eyes widening as he started putting two and two together. Zombie cow. Zombie Bart. Zombie burgers. Zombie crowd.

He started nodding. "It looks like you're going to need more than one slugger."

"We could be wrong, you know," Joe said. "We don't know that the meat will really do anything.... We could be totally wrong."

"We could be," Miguel said. "But I don't think we are...."

It happened slowly at first. A lady on the hillside flopped over, clutching her throat. Then there was another burst of excitement—it looked like a couple of people were getting into some kind of wrestling fight. One guy grabbed another and dragged him down.

If you didn't know what you were looking for, it just looked like some people—one here, a couple there—starting to push or grab at the others, but it was kind of like when a crowd does the wave. It starts somewhere, and it ripples out—*whoosh, whoosh, whoosh*, pushing through the crowd. More and more people, dropping their burgers and grabbing their neighbors instead.

Someone started screaming. An old guy had latched onto a big muscle-y dude's head with his teeth and the big guy was trying to shake him off. People were jumping up and looking around, confused. More fights broke out, and more and more people started biting one another. A chorus of screams rose from the stands.

Officer Baby Face had grabbed some lady and was

trying to wrestle her off her husband, but she was chewing into the guy's arm.

And then came the sound I dreaded.

"Brraaaaiiiinnnsssss."

A keening moan, shimmering in the hot Iowa air. The promise of mayhem.

The kids on the other baseball team all turned to look up at the fighting, shading their eyes in the bright sunshine.

Sammy's dad was standing right beside us, chewing on a burger. I did a double take.

"Where'd he get that?" I asked, but it was too late to do anything about it.

More and more people were running around, moaning and groaning for brains. I saw a guy dashing for the parking lot with two little girls hanging onto his legs, gnawing away. Talk about ankle biters. A mom was chasing her kid, trying to bite him. An old grandpa grabbed a grandma and chomped down on her shoulder.

The zombie plague was spreading, and it was happening fast. Even faster than when people got bit. The zombie meat seemed to change them almost right away.

"We got to get out of here," Miguel said.

"There's a lot of zombies between us and the truck," I said.

At that moment the zombies noticed us down on the baseball field.

"Here they come," Joe murmured. "Better think of something fast."

"There's too many to fight!" Miguel said. "Look at all of them!"

The crowd of hungry zombies had definitely sniffed out the fresh meat of us players down on the baseball diamond. A couple of them were already stumbling down the hill, and it was just a matter of time before the trickle of zombies became a tsunami.

"We're dead," Joe said as he grabbed a baseball bat. "Guess this is it."

There were too many to get through easily. We needed some kind of a plan, but everybody was confused—or, like Joe, they were just planning on going down swinging.

Well, you always said you wanted to be the strategy guy.

I took a deep breath and jumped up on the bench. "Hey, everyone! Listen to me! I got a plan!"

But, of course, no one listened. The players were pointing at the mayhem up on the hill and asking one another what the heck was going on, or saying things like, "Is that your mom biting your dad?" Some of them had walked out onto the diamond to get a better view as they tried to figure it out. But no one was listening to me.

"Listen up!" I shouted. "They're zombies! I got a plan!"

No one heard me.

"Here, man. I got this," a voice said behind me.

Otis climbed up beside me and stuck his fingers in his mouth. He whistled so loudly my eardrums almost popped. Everyone's heads whipped around.

Otis shouted, "Listen up, you all! Rabi's got something to say. Those people up there are turning into zombies, and we got to get out of here. And Rabi's got the plan for how we're gonna do it. So shut up and listen, or I'll kick all your butts!"

And just like that, all eyes turned to me.

I froze like a rabbit.

"Come on, Rabi," Miguel whispered.

"Right," I said. I cleared my throat. "Right." My voice was still stuck. I tried again, making my voice loud. Trying to make it confident. Like Joe, when he'd pretended on the phone. Pretending to be a leader, so that I could *be* the leader.

"Okay, guys! If we try to run and we don't work together, we're going to get caught, and we're going to get chewed to pieces, just like all the people up there. We need to get through those zombies and—"

"Who says they're zombies?" Sammy challenged.

At that moment we heard gunshots. We all looked up. Officer Boone was surrounded by zombies. He fired again—*Bang! Bang!*—double-tap to a zombie's head.

The zombie didn't even slow down. It just grabbed him and started chewing. Everyone gasped as Officer Baby Face went down screaming.

"Any other doubters?" I asked.

In the silence that followed, Sammy's dad said, "Come on, Sammy. We've got to get out of here."

"You can't!" I said. "We've got to stick together!"

But Mr. Riggoni was already striding away, his son in tow. "He ate the burger!" I shouted after Sammy, but Sammy wasn't listening; he was running. And I could tell the others were thinking about running, too. Scattering like a bunch of scared chickens. I was going to lose them to panic in two seconds.

Pretend you're the coach. Act like you're in charge.

If Sammy's dumb dad could get people to listen to him when he was wrong, I should have been able to get them to listen when I was right. I straightened up, tall.

"All right, guys! If we're going to get out of here, we got to stay organized. The one advantage we got over zombies is that they're *dumb*. They can't think their way out of a paper bag. Dumber than Sammy's dad, right? So if we stay tight, and we work together, we can get through this," I shouted. "You hear me?"

I heard a mutter.

"Are we going to stay *organized*?" I shouted.

Otis understood what I was trying to do. "Yes!" he shouted.

"We staying tight?" I shouted.

More guys called out. "Yeah!"

"Zombies got no brains, but we got ours, and we got each other, and we're getting out of here!" I shouted. *"You hear me?"*

"Yeah!"

"Okay! Get your balls and bats, guys: We're playing us some zombie baseball."

In front of me, I could see all my teammates and their baseball skills. Jason, who was quiet but hit singles all day long. Otis, who could clear a fence when he hit hard. Joe, who swung hard but was always wild. Amos, who had a killer fastball. Miguel, who never flinched from a pitch, and hit like a freight train. Sid Meacham, who could throw a ball from deep right field and get it to third. More and more players. I could see their stats running through my head.

Screams and shouts echoed down from the stands, but it seemed distant to me. All I cared about was fastballs and home runs and singles and sliders, and left-handed batters and right-handed batters. I was organizing them in my head as fast as I could, solving the weirdest math problem in the world, looking for power from my forward players, to knock zombies aside; speed from the backups, who could pop a zombie if someone missed....

"First things first," I shouted. "Don't try to kill the zombies! You saw what happened with the cop and the gun. Maybe there's some way to kill 'em, but we don't know what it is."

"So what do we do?" someone asked.

"I'm going to tell you! Rule One: Don't get bit! Rule Two: Go for the knees! A crippled zombie is too slow to matter! Rule Three: Keep moving!"

The zombies were shambling toward us, smelling a whole team of fresh meat down on the baseball field, and now they were really starting to charge: one, and then three, now a dozen, now...

"They're coming!" Otis shouted.

I needed more time. Miguel seemed to read my mind. He strode out and nailed a leading zombie in the knees.

Whack! Whack!

The zombie went down, but there were a heck of a lot

more behind it. Otis joined Miguel as I scrambled to organize the team on the field. I wished I could have kept my bat, but I wasn't a slugger, so I handed it off to Jaz Zodrow, who was bigger and better.

"You better not let me get bit," I said.

He grinned. "Don't worry. Zombies are way bigger than baseballs."

"Where are we going?" Sid asked as I got him positioned.

I pointed at the onrushing zombie horde. "Right through them."

Sid's eyes widened with fear. "You can't be serious."

I glanced over my shoulder; it was worse than I thought.

Wall-to-wall zombies.

Otis and Miguel had given up on holding off the horde, and were bolting back to the safety of the group. I cupped my hands around my mouth. "We're going to be a wedge! We got a pickup truck up there in the lot, but we got to get through all these zombies first!" I shouted.

"Miguel's up front! Otis and Eddie are with him! Travis and Tommy, you guys are backup. Pitchers are in the middle. You see someone in trouble, you bean their zombie, hard! Me and Campbell and Steven, we're on ball duty. We're going to keep the pitchers loaded, right?

"Remember—we keep moving, we stay together, and we keep an eye on our buddies. Zombies are just dumb meat with legs. We got the advantage, 'cause we work together."

Miguel hefted his bat. "Good speech, buddy. Let's hope you're right."

"Here they come!" someone shouted.

"*Charge!*" I shouted. "Show 'em what we got!"

CHAPTER 36

We went up the hill like a fighter jet, a wedge of whistling baseball bats and killer fastballs.

The zombies came down on us like a tsunami.

When we hit, I thought we were going down. A tidal wave of hungry monsters poured over us. I didn't think we'd hold. Miguel and Otis and Eddie were screaming and swinging like crazy, smashing and slamming zombies aside. Miguel anchored the point, switch-hitting on every swing like he'd been born to do it. Eddie and Otis backed him, swinging lefty and righty, pounding zombies aside and clearing space for us to keep up the charge.

Man, there were *a lot* of them.

"Don't fight them!" I ordered as more zombies poured down on us. "Bounce 'em to the side and keep us moving!"

Knee-cracking, head-smacking, baseball bats flying, we bashed our way forward, whacking zombies aside. We fought for every step, gaining speed as we hammered through, charging forward now, faster up the hill, everyone working together—

A zombie got around the side of our wedge and dove in from the rear. I shoved my baseball glove into its face. The zombie bit down, but there weren't any fingers to chew there. Then Jaz whacked it upside the head with the baseball bat I'd loaned him, and the zombie went down.

"Thanks, man!"

"Nice bat" was all Jaz said as he swung again and knocked another zombie down. A baseball whistled past my ear and clocked a zombie lady who was trying to get at Miguel from his blind side. Another one followed, nailing a zombie that had been about to lunge in on Otis as he tangled with another.

"Keep moving!"

I saw that the other baseball team was taking my strategy, too, charging up the hill to the bus that they'd ridden in on.

"Do we want the bus?" Joe shouted as he whacked another zombie's leg out from under it with a *crack*.

"*No!* Keep moving. We can swing better if we're on the truck! And there's no telling if the bus driver's even alive!"

We broke through the initial wave of zombies and kept hacking our way up the slope to the parking lot.

I could see some people who weren't bitten were still running around. Some blond girl with long legs was just outrunning the suckers. She scooped up a little kid as she ran. She saw us and angled toward us.

"Let her in!" I shouted.

She hurtled into our midst, gasping. "Thanks!" she said.

The little kid was crying. "Either of you get bit?" I asked.

She shook her head. "From zombies? No way. Soon as I saw the first one try to bite, I knew what was up."

Joe swung his bat into another zombie kneecap. "You read comics?"

"I play *Left 4 Dead*," she said as she scooped up some old lady's cane and rammed it into a zombie's eye.

Joe was staring at the girl with total love. I swear he almost got bit. Otis had to whack a zombie in the face, just to get us past.

We kept moving. The pitchers ran out of balls, so I got down with the little kid and said to her, "If you see hard things like bottles and soda cans, you give 'em to us, so we can throw them, okay? Just pick 'em up and give 'em to our pitchers, okay? That's what I'm doing."

She wiped her eyes and got to work, picking up whatever she could find. I grabbed a lawn chair and heaved it into some more zombies that were sneaking up behind us, and tossed a bottle to the pitchers. A full soda can clocked another zombie in the nose.

We made it up the hill and across the parking lot, and the zombies... well, they spent half their time trying to eat one another, half their time chasing us, and half their time wandering around in circles, and if you think that doesn't add up, you're right—zombies are some confused, stupid monsters when it comes down to it.

We made it to the truck. "Sluggers in the truck bed!" I shouted.

"*Aaah!*" someone yelled. "There's a cow head in here!"

Everyone started flipping out. "Get it out! Get it out!"

Joe ran up. "Gimme that!"

He grabbed Bart the Zombie Cow. The head mooed and snapped at him, but he kept his fingers free.

Everyone piled into the back of the truck. Miguel jumped into the driver's side and started up the engine. The roar of the truck attracted the zombies again, like they realized we were about to get away. They charged after us just as I was shoving the last of the baseball team up into the truck.

"Bats on the outside!" I shouted.

I did a quick count, it looked like we had everyone except—

Where was Joe?

"Hey, Rabi! Check it out!"

Joe was standing in front of the truck, grinning. A zombie came staggering toward him.

"Watch out!" I shouted.

He turned and swung his bat.

One! Two!

Kneecaps.

The zombie went down. Good swings, too. Super-clean. Joe wasn't swinging anywhere near as wild as he did in the games. Zombies had a way of focusing the mind, I guessed.

"Come here!" Joe said, still grinning.

"Will you get in the truck!" I shouted.

"Yeah, in a minute! Check this out!"

I went around to the front.

Bart the Zombie Cow stared at me and bared his teeth, mooing. Joe had jammed the head onto the bumper of the truck, so that it stuck there like some kind of crazed mascot, glowering and snapping.

"MOOOOOoooooooo!" Bart said, clearly mad that Joe had turned him into a hood ornament.

"Awesome, right?" Joe was grinning.

It was the zombie apocalypse and our town was falling apart, but I couldn't help laughing. I shoved Joe toward the door. "Get in the truck, you nut job."

We piled into the cab and slammed the doors. Miguel gunned the engine again, and the zombies seemed to redouble their efforts to chew into our living flesh. A huge wave of them charged toward us.

"Drive!" I shouted.

But we didn't. Instead, Miguel started fiddling with the controls on the truck.

"What are you doing?" I shouted.

"Putting it in four."

"Are you kidding?" I asked. "Let's go!"

A light flicked green on the dashboard: 4WD.

Miguel nodded in satisfaction and gunned the engine. We roared toward the wall of zombies as they came in at us.

"Everybody brace!" I shouted, but it looked like Otis had already warned the team in back, because everyone was crouching.

The zombies rushed forward. Miguel floored the gas.

As we hit, I could have sworn I heard Bart the Zombie Cow mooing with delight.

CHAPTER 37

Zombie splatter. Big-time.

We smashed into the horde and the truck jerked and we all bounced off the dashboard. But Miguel kept the gas on, and then that big old Ford F-250 was climbing up and over all those zombies, crunching and bouncing, four-wheel-drive fully engaged, engine roaring.

It was just like a monster truck rally, the way we plowed through zombies. Joe was shouting and cheering, and the rest of the team in the back had their bats out, beating back the zombies that were trying to board us from the sides. The truck smashed through the last of the standing zombies and crunched over the rest, and Miguel floored it again.

Behind us, we left a trail of smushed zombies, like

we'd driven through a cornfield and just mowed it down. For a second, you could see exactly where we'd driven, and then more zombies stumbled into the cleared space, and our trail disappeared under a fresh mob of brain-starved undead.

As we peeled out of the parking lot, we saw other zombies wandering around on the streets, too. It looked like Milrow had put their meat out all over the place, because the town wasn't looking too great. I wondered if all the trucks had delivered meat to our town, or if there were zombie uprisings happening in other places, too.

We roared down Grand Avenue, not pausing for the stoplights. Ahead, a couple of people were being chased by zombies.

"Is that Sammy and his dad?" Joe asked.

I squinted. Sure enough, that's who it was. They were running, and four or five zombies were chasing after them.

"Should we stop and help?" Joe asked.

I looked over at Miguel.

"We stopping?" I asked him.

Miguel shook his head. "I don't see any reason."

I hesitated, then said, "Come on. They're still people."

"They *say* they're people." Miguel kept his hands firm

on the wheel. "But they never treated me or my family like anything other than dogs."

"But...they're *people*."

"Just because they walk around and they've got two hands and two feet, that don't make them people. People help each other out," Miguel said. "Like Otis, right? People don't eat each other up and throw each other away. Those two? They were always zombies. They just didn't know it."

Sammy was waving and calling out. His dad—

"Dang," I said. "His dad is chasing him, too. His dad's already a zombie."

"Sammy'll never make it if we don't stop," Joe sighed. "I hate to say it, but I think maybe we ought to show pity on the sucker."

I looked from Joe to Miguel, not knowing how to feel.

Sammy had definitely been terrible to us since forever. Sammy had acted like we weren't even people. He'd told us we didn't belong. I thought about all the things he'd called us over the years, and all the crummy things he'd done. When his dad did terrible things to Miguel and his family, Sammy had gloated about it.

I didn't like Sammy at all.

I sighed. "Slow down, Miguel."

Miguel glanced over. "Are you kidding?"

"No. I guess not."

Miguel's face hardened. "Nope. I'm not doing it."

"Come on, Miguel. You're better than he is. We're all better than he is. Even on our worst day, we're better than Sammy. Don't play it the way he would."

For a second, I wasn't sure that I could get through, but then Miguel let out his breath slowly and took his foot off the gas. You could see Sammy's relief as we slowed and he managed to catch up to us.

"Roll down the window," I said. "But keep moving."

Sammy caught up to the window, clutching its edge. "Thank you thank you thank you—"

He saw who was driving and recoiled.

I grinned at him. "You sure you want to get in the truck?" I asked.

"Yes! Just lemme in! My dad's a zombie!"

"Yeah, well, he kind of brought that on himself," Miguel said.

The zombies were gaining on us.

"You sorry for all the things you said to us?" I asked.

Sammy was nodding like a dashboard bobblehead. "Yeah! Yeah! I'm sorry!"

"Tell me you love Mexicans!"

"I love Mexicans!"

"Tell me you love immigrants!"

"I love immigrants!"

I looked at Joe and Miguel. "You think he's telling the truth? Or you think he's just trying to get a ride?"

Joe looked at me with a sparkle in his eye. "I dunno. I don't really buy it."

"Me, either," Miguel said.

I looked at Sammy. "Sorry, man. They don't believe you."

"Please!" he said. "Pleasepleasepleasepleaseplease."

He was pathetic.

When he'd been on top, he'd treated us like dirt. Now that he was on the bottom, he'd turned into jelly. No spine at all. Just a rich kid who lived the good life and then one day looked around and found out that he needed other people to stay alive after all.

"You get one chance," I said to him, and then I shouted over my shoulder to the kids in the back, "Let him up!"

"Are we sure about this?" Miguel asked. "He really is bad news."

"Maybe he learned a lesson," I said.

"Maybe he didn't."

"So we'll watch him," I said. "If he doesn't straighten

up, we can always toss him back to the zombies later. No reason we have to keep putting up with bad behavior. Not anymore."

The rest of the team was hauling Sammy up into the truck bed. We gunned the engine and headed for the open road, zooming through cornfields, headed for where, I didn't know.

Who knew what kind of life we'd find? Who knew how far the zombie apocalypse was spreading?

But I was glad I had my friends with me, and a team behind me, and whatever happened, I figured that between all of us working together, we'd get it sorted out.

EPILOGUE

"You mean we can't talk about this to anyone?"

We were all sitting in a big old conference room in a big old skyscraper in big old Chicago. We had a view of other huge skyscrapers, and if you put your face to the glass, you could see down all the way to the cars, little tiny toys below.

But I wasn't looking at the view.

I was sitting at the table with my mom and dad, Miguel, Joe, Joe's mom, and our lawyer. And across the table from us sat Lawrence Maximillian, the cold-blooded lizard lawyer of Milrow Meat Solutions.

And he was smiling.

Maximillian looked at me over his little rectangular glasses. "Rabi, you're in possession of proprietary company information. It's not yours to share. It never was."

"But you guys were breaking the rules! This whole thing only happened because you were doing bad things with your cows! All those zombie outbreaks? They had to call out the National Guard in six different towns!"

Maximillian looked at me. "Don't be hysterical. They were small towns. In any case, you signed nondisclosure agreements."

Our lawyer cleared his throat. "Those agreements were signed without anything approaching full consent. The boys are minors."

"I should sue you for even coming close to my kid," my dad said.

"Consider your position very carefully," Maximillian said. "Going to trial is risky business. If I end up seeing you in court, I'll crush you with court costs. And if I win, I will take away everything that you have earned or ever will earn."

"But we didn't do anything wrong!" Joe's mom protested.

"No?" Maximillian's eyebrows rose. He started ticking points off on his fingers. "You left young children unattended. Said children trespassed. Said children stole from a meatpacking facility—"

"You mean the cow head that wouldn't die," Miguel interjected.

"—They assaulted a Milrow employee—"

"Mr. Cocoran was trying to eat our brains!" Joe protested.

Maximillian was still ticking off charges. "So: theft, trespassing, assault. Not to mention the fact that your children were roaming free in a meat-processing facility, a very dangerous environment. I'll bet I can bury you on child endangerment and neglect alone. By the time I'm done, I might even have custody of your children."

My mom had had enough. "Our boys were driving around in a pickup for a week, fighting creatures that came from your meatpacking plant. I'd be happy to see you in court!"

"Don't be so eager for a trial, Mrs. Chatterjee. I've never lost a major case, and, frankly, we can afford to drag something like this out for years. And consider this: If by some chance you finally win some minor complaint against us, well, Milrow Meat Solutions will simply file for bankruptcy. The day after that, another company will buy our facilities and hire our personnel, and we'll all go right back to our jobs. You'll change nothing. You can't kill a company like Milrow, and you can't hurt us. But in the meantime, we can hurt you a great deal."

My parents were starting to look ill at the threats, but I wasn't going to roll over to Larry Max this time. "We've still got the videos that Joe took. All those zombie cows? All your cleanup squad workers chopping up the cows and sending them out for people to eat? We have proof!"

Maximillian smiled. "Sadly, taking secret videos on a farm is terribly illegal. There are civil and criminal penalties. Fines. Jail time. You can't just waltz onto a farm and take videos of things you're not supposed to see. We've worked hard to pass farm-protection laws in many states, for just these sorts of criminal intrusions."

"You're not a farm!"

"Just because Milrow Meat Solutions is large doesn't mean it doesn't deserve to be protected from activists and troublemakers."

"You broke the law!" I said.

"Actually, there are very few laws that have been broken. Accidents happen, that's all. It's a sad thing when accidents happen, but that's all this was."

"You sold bad meat to people."

"Well, it's possible that a rogue executive like Mr. Riggoni is probably liable for unethical decisions." Maximillian grinned. "But he'll be in a cage for life, muttering for brains. I don't see how you could punish him any more."

"But it was your cleanup squad who put all the meat

in the trucks and shipped it out. Somebody at Milrow ordered that. Maybe you, even."

Maximillian spread his hands, still smiling. "I can only tell you what our internal investigations have concluded: no evidence of conspiracy or criminal neglect. The USDA and FDA have already addressed the safety concerns related to beef feed, growth hormones, antibiotic use, et cetera, et cetera, et cetera, and they're fully satisfied that we meet national health and safety guidelines for beef production. Milrow Meat Solutions has fired the responsible personnel, and there is a voluntary, ongoing, and thorough internal review of our food-safety practices. We have already determined who the main culprits were, but unfortunately the majority of the lawbreakers were removed across the border by Immigration and Customs Enforcement just before the outbreak, so certain legal remedies are not available."

Maximillian used big words, and he talked like he was a real person, but if you read between the lines, it was pure evil that he was saying. And you could tell that he knew it, and didn't care.

"You mean people like Miguel's aunt and uncle," I said. "You're trying to blame the regular workers."

"Lax hiring practices on senior executive Riggoni's part resulted in unforeseen manufacturing difficulties, and rogue employee decision making. I think that's the line we'll be taking."

Which meant that they really were going to blame a bunch of innocent people for something that some rich dude in a skyscraper had decided would make some extra money.

I stood up. "You suck. You all suck. It was your fault, and you know it. You're the ones who put all the weird stuff in the cow food, and gave them the weird shots, and left all those cows out there in those feedlots, getting sick. Miguel's uncle saw all kinds of nasty things—"

"All perfectly acceptable, according to the U.S. Department of Agriculture—"

"—and now you want to lay this on someone else and cover it all up, and call it an E. coli outbreak. There's some rich guy in Des Moines, or Chicago, or Omaha, or New York City, or something, and he's sitting back and making all kinds of money while he throws good people out of America and feeds us all his bad meat."

Phew. That was some kind of major speech. I looked around the table. My friends were nodding. Even our parents were nodding.

Joe said, "We've already decided. We're going to upload the whole video from the inside of your meat-packing plant, and then everyone's going to know what you guys were doing. We're going to let people see what they think of the way you make meat in Delbe."

Maximillian said, "Alas. We've already closed the plant. It should have been closed down years ago. It was much too small, anyway. We've got bigger, better, state-of-the-art beef-processing facilities now." He leaned forward. "And let me tell you, if you distribute that video, don't forget it's been illegally obtained. We will, of course, sue, and the full force of this corporation will take your money, your homes, everything...."

Miguel crossed his arms, not looking impressed. "So, what if *I* do it?" he asked. "What are you going to take from me that you haven't taken already? You already sicced ICE on my mom, my dad, my aunt, my uncle. I don't even have a home. I'm living at Rabi's house now, and don't even know if I get to stay. How about I pay you back for all that?"

For the first time, fear flickered in Maximillian's eyes. "Miguel," he said soothingly. "I thought we had an arrangement. I know you want to stay in this country...."

"I want my family back," Miguel said. "And I want them to be citizens."

"Miguel..."

"And me, too. I want full citizenship."

"ICE is notoriously difficult—"

287

"ICE never raids unless you ask for it. ICE does whatever you big-money guys want. You told us before that you have senators in your pocket. So? What's it going to be?"

"All right, all right." Maximillian caved. "We'll work something out."

Miguel shook his head. "Nope. I was just fooling with you. No deals. Not with you guys. Not anymore. You don't make me roll over. Never again. I'm not taking a single thing from your dirty hands."

And the way he said it, he was ice-cold. Stronger than I'd ever seen him. He'd always been stand-up, but now, it was like he owned Lawrence Maximillian. There wasn't a bit of fear in Miguel.

And Maximillian was suddenly terrified, because he'd run into the first person in his life who couldn't be bought.

Miguel was without question the most heroic guy I had ever met. I wanted to stand up and cheer. Even when it would have been easier for him, he wasn't going to let up. Even if we were all covering for ourselves, and afraid, he was willing to go the full distance. Even if it got him deported to Mexico, he was going to do it.

Except, I really didn't want my best friend to get kicked out of the country, and it looked like that was about to happen.

I started thinking furiously, trying to come up with

some way to get Miguel to just take the deal. *Let it go.* But I knew he wouldn't. Miguel was too ethical for his own good. And then it hit me.

"Miguel." I pulled him aside, whispering, "I got an idea."

"What's that?"

"I got an idea. Something that gets your parents back."

"I don't care. I'm bringing Milrow down. That's what I want. I'm not making a deal with those devils."

"Yeah, I know. I agree. But, listen, we don't need the pictures or the video. We got something else."

"What's that?"

"A story."

He gave me a puzzled look. "A story? What's that supposed to mean?"

"Look. As soon as that video goes up, what's Milrow going to do? They're going to say it's fake. They're going to sue anyone who puts it up. They'll make people take it down. Maybe some people will see it, but Maximillian and his goons will make it seem like it's stupid movie footage. Not the real thing."

"So? It's all we got. And I'm going to use it."

"I'm saying we got something better. And Milrow won't be able to do a single thing about it. We've just got to make sure the lawyers draw up the agreements in the right way. We'll agree that we won't ever release the videos, in return for Milrow getting your family back into the country, and getting you citizenship."

"No! Then we're giving up—"

"And we won't talk to the press, and we won't go on TV...."

"I won't do that!"

"Will you listen to me? We got something better. We got a story, right? Just a story. A harmless little story about some kids who were playing baseball one day, and then there were these strange cows, and then their hometown started to go weird. I bet a lot of people would like hearing a crazy story like that." I shrugged. "Especially if it's just a story. Milrow won't be able to do anything about a story, right?"

Miguel had started smiling.

"You with me?" I asked.

"Oh yeah. One hundred percent."

We came back to the table. "We'll do your deal, Maximillian. We're all in."

* * *

The thing I realized while we were talking at the lawyer's table was that Milrow Meat Solutions would sue us to death for telling the truth. They'd sue for showing videos of the truth. They'd make all kinds of trouble about the *truth*. They really could take away our house and all that kind of stuff, but there was one way, maybe, they couldn't.

And that's if we made the whole thing up.

So here you've got this book in your hands, and I'm telling you—straight up and down—that I made this whole story up. The zombies and Milrow and everything in it. I made up the names and the places and everything. Any resemblance to real people, real things, or real events is purely coincidental—I think that's how the lawyers like to say it.

I'm telling you that there *wasn't* a zombie uprising, and my friends and I *didn't* beat them down with baseball bats. And, of course, Milrow Meat Solutions didn't cut corners and stuff their cows with all kinds of weird drugs and nasty feed. And for sure, they didn't sweep their zombie scandal under the rug and call it an E. coli scare.

None of that. Nope. Didn't happen.

This is fiction, right? Just a scary story with some thrills and chills. I swear to you that Bart the Zombie Cow Head isn't hanging on the wall in Joe's room, mooing in the dark, while Joe reads his comics with a flashlight.

But, you know what else?

Sometimes, truth is even stranger than fiction.

Oops. My lawyers just told me I can't say that.

So maybe I'll just say instead that grown-ups tell us all kinds of things. They tell us what's true and what's not; and they tell us they're responsible, even when they're out to lunch; and they tell us how things are safe when a lot of times they aren't; but most of all, they tell you what *never ever* happens, because it would be *impossible*.

But you know how a pitcher pretends he's going to throw a fastball, and then he switches up and throws a curve instead?

At the end of the day, it's up to us to not get fooled by the things grown-ups throw at us. And it's up to you, right now, to read between the lines. And sometimes, it's up to all of us to take the zombies down.

If we all stick together, it's possible. We don't have to let the bad guys win. Working together, we can do anything.

That's the real truth.

Your friend always,

Rabi

Rabindranath Chatterjee-Jones

ACKNOWLEDGMENTS

I'd very much like to thank Holly Black and Cassie Claire for letting me tag along on a retreat to Mexico, and for giving me the time and space away from the regular world to dream up Rabi's. I also have to thank Holly for repeated inspiration when I stalled out and didn't know where to go next; her support was critical and helped me keep faith as I hacked through my initial draft. I'd particularly like to thank Jobim for getting this idea started; without him, I never would have considered writing about zombies. Andrea Spooner, my fabulous editor, was instrumental in making this book sharper, smarter, and more fun. For help with baseball authenticity, Gary Russell and Jason Nicholoff were instrumental. I also owe Rob Ziegler for some early all-American inspiration. Many thanks to Anu Bandopadhay for her help with Bengali, and Juan Diego Gomez and Jennie Chavez for help with my terrible Spanish. I'd also like to thank Greg VanEekhout for help with comics knowledge, and Sarah Prineas for help with Iowa cornfields, and a heck of a lot of wisdom along the way, not just on this book, but on all of them.

And of course, Rabi and I would like to thank major meat-processing corporations worldwide for their continued inspiration. It's always nice to pick up a newspaper and read about another E. coli outbreak.

Errors, omissions, flops, and failures, as usual, are my own.

DISCUSSION GUIDE

1. Who are your favorite and least favorite characters in *Zombie Baseball Beatdown*? Why?

2. Rabi, Miguel, and Joe are close friends, but Miguel withholds information about the true status of his citizenship from Rabi and Joe. Why, do you think, does he do this? Do you think it was right for him not to tell his friends?

3. Friendship is an important theme in this story. How do the characters show that they are good friends to one another? When are they not good friends to one another?

4. The adults in the story are a big problem for the boys because they don't believe their story or aren't around to help. How do you deal with adults who won't listen to you? What kinds of things can kids do that adults can't?

5. In this story, all three boys have "superpowers" that make them a winning team. Rabi uses his brain to figure out their plan, Miguel uses his strength to keep the zombies (and bullies) from hurting them, and Joe uses his looks to blend in when they don't want to be seen. Which of these powers would you want to have? What's another superpower that an ordinary kid could have?

6. Even though this story is set in a small community in Iowa, some of the issues presented throughout the book are problems that people face all over the United States and even around the world. Which issues made an impact on you and why?

7. What do you think it means to be "American"? How do you think the different characters in this book would answer this question? Would Rabi's answer be different from Miguel's? What would Sammy say?

8. Even though it puts them in danger, members of Miguel's family speak up about the conditions at the meatpacking plant. Do you think they made the right decision? Why or why not?

9. Do you ever wonder about where the food you eat comes from? What other questions did this book make you ask yourself?

10. Do you think you would survive a zombie apocalypse? What do Rabi, Miguel, and Joe do to protect themselves, and what things would you do that they didn't?

AN INTERVIEW WITH PAOLO BACIGALUPI

This is your first novel for middle grade readers. What made you decide to write a story for this age group?

Well, once upon a time, there was a boy who hated reading but loved zombies....

More seriously, I wanted to write for young people because my wife is a schoolteacher, and I hear a lot about how kids feel about the books they have to read. And the thing that stands out to me again and again is how boring a lot of assigned books sound. In the case of *Zombie Baseball Beatdown*, I wanted to give a kid in my wife's class a story that would let him know that books don't have to be a dry sawdust sandwich. Books can be a joy, and they can have zombie battles and sports and mystery and teamwork and all the fun that a video game or a movie might have. Books don't have to be boring. I wanted to give a kid an awesome reading experience.

How is it different to write for young readers as opposed to writing for adults?

It's more fun, and I like my characters more. My kid characters tend to be smart and funny and likable in ways that my adult writing doesn't allow. I also tend to laugh more when I'm writing for young readers. There's a sense of glee that you get when you write about a zombie chasing kids through a cornfield and a sort of "heh, heh, heh, and THEN THE ZOMBIE JUMPS OUT!" feeling to the whole enterprise that has me eagerly anticipating how I'm going to surprise my reader next. And that means that writing stories like *Zombie Baseball Beatdown* is more of a joy for me than when I write for adults. There's more of a sense of fun and humanity and play in these books.

Where did you come up with the idea for Zombie Baseball Beatdown?

It started with that student I mentioned before. He wanted to read about zombies. And I knew that he didn't mean the cute and fuzzy zombies who just need a hug that I've seen in young people's fiction, but real zombies that were really dangerous. Of course, once you've got zombies, you need weapons...and somehow baseball bats just seemed perfect and easily available to kids in middle school. Once you've got a bunch of kids with baseball bats and a bunch of zombies, the beatdown takes care of itself.

Do you relate to one of the characters in this book more than the others? Which one are you the most similar to?

I relate most strongly to Rabi. In many ways he's based on my son, who is also a half-Indian kid growing up in the middle of rural nowhere.

There are a number of complex issues in this book that readers may have firsthand knowledge of, or may have never thought about before. What do you hope readers will take away from the story?

First and foremost, I hope they enjoy reading the story. If they don't, I haven't done my job. Beyond that? I hope they come away with a sense of empathy for people who seem different from them, and who live in different circumstances than they do. And of course, I also hope that they have a chance to think a little bit about where their food comes from. All our industrial food companies spend so much time trying to obscure the day-to-day reality of what they do that it seems important that we scrutinize them closely.

What kind of research did you do before writing about the themes in this book like immigration, food safety, and baseball? Did you have to study zombie lore to make sure you were creating authentic monsters?

I was already pretty familiar with industrial meatpacking, and I was also pretty aware of issues related to growing up as a minority in America thanks to my wife and son. For sure, an early inspiration was Eric Schlosser's book *Fast Food Nation*. The book is nonfiction, but you could also probably classify it as horror. For the immigration research, I ended up reading a lot of firsthand accounts of living without documentation in the United States, reading through the history of our laws related to immigration and our current political gridlock over these issues. And then, of course, there is a steady stream of news stories that you can read. If you look, there's a lot of information out there. Mostly we don't look and don't pay attention, which is tragic because immigration is a complex topic and deserves our attention. As for zombies, I took the parts of the zombie canon that worked for the story I wanted to tell. One of the fun things about using a pop-culture element like zombies is how much these monsters have been mixed and remixed over time. It gives you a lot of room to play.

What advice would you give to aspiring writers?

1) You have to be tenacious. It's possible to become a writer, but only if you never give up. You have to face failure and rejections and complicated plot problems and hard revisions, and only the people who keep at the work ever break through. All the writers I know who are successful also have stories about how hard it was for them to break into the writing business. They kept going, despite the fact that it felt nearly impossible at the time.

2) You have to always be learning and always be seeking to improve your writing. If you can keep learning to write better and keep learning how to tell better stories, and if you keep trying out new ways of writing stories, it means that you won't get stuck in a rut. And even though your first book won't sell, it means that your fifth book can. That's what happened to me. Because I was always learning and always improving my writing, and because I never quit, I eventually made it. It was hard work getting here, but now it's quite a lot of fun.

HOW TO SURVIVE THE (NEXT) ZOMBIE APOCALYPSE

The zombie apocalypse hit my Iowa town.

WHAT WILL YOU DO WHEN IT HITS YOURS?

Here's what *you* can do to prepare for a zombie outbreak in ten simple steps.

1: KNOW THE FACTS.

The possibility of a zombie outbreak in your town increases:

near polluted areas.[1]

if it enters the food supply.[2]

if you're within fifty feet of my Little League coach, Mr. Cocoran (aka Patient Zero).[3]

This is because contaminated areas are *zombie breeding grounds*!

70%

of evil monsters come
from nasty places like
toxic waste dumps.[4]

100%

of documented zombie
outbreaks originated from
an infected food supply.[5]

2: READ.

Readers of zombie literature are more likely to survive the apocalypse than those who focus on all other subjects combined.[6] Everything you need to know about zombies can be learned from zombie books, comics, and blogs.

3: PROTECT YOUR HEAD.

To a zombie, your brain tastes like the best food ever.[7]

9 OUT OF 10 ZOMBIES say they prefer brains to any other food.[8]

The brain size of kids who like **READING IS 1/10 LARGER** than that of kids who don't.[9]

On average, zombies find **BIGGER BRAINS 33%** more appetizing than small brains.[10]

4: USE YOUR HEAD.

Know how to problem solve because zombies are a big problem. For instance:

IF 23 ZOMBIE COWS ARE BLOCKING THE EXIT...

AND I'VE GOT 2 FRIENDS WITH ME, WHO CAN EACH TAKE DOWN 1 ZOMBIE COW IN 45 SECONDS...

HOW LONG WILL IT TAKE TO BRING DOWN THE ENTIRE HERD?

2 + 2 = BRAINS

Extensive research has shown that **98% OF ZOMBIES ARE UNABLE TO SOLVE SIMPLE MATHEMATICAL EQUATIONS** giving you a significant advantage.[11]

5: PLAY BASEBALL.

A field study found that when it comes to disabling zombies with sports equipment, it took:

3 SWINGS
of a baseball bat.[12]

6 SWINGS
of a hockey stick.[13]

4,587 SWINGS
(AND SEVERAL STABS)
of a Ping-Pong paddle.[14]

So play baseball! It sharpens your aim and targeting skills, and those are useful because zombies can be as surprising as a mean curveball. Plus baseball teaches you to work with a team, and you will definitely need to work with all your buddies to defeat zombies. *No one survives alone.*

6: ARMOR UP!

A focus group of zombies who had at least six or more teeth revealed:

• 92% were easily able to bite through a single layer of clothing, penetrating the skin.

• 33% were unable to bite through five or more layers of clothing.

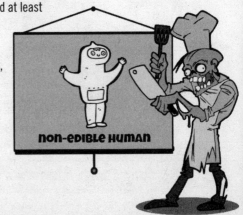

NON-EDIBLE HUMAN

Zombies hang on like ticks, so wear as many layers of clothes as you can. There's no shame in looking like a marshmallow man when you're battling zombies![15]

7: PLAY *DANCE DANCE REVOLUTION.*

The music video game teaches valuable jumping, dodging, and shuffling skills learned nowhere else.[16]

80% of kids who excel at *DDR* were able to effortlessly dodge a zombie's swiping hands & clumsy grabs.

AND FINALLY, STAY ALERT!

8: KEEP YOUR EYES PEELED FOR CLOUDS OF FLIES!

9: KEEP YOUR EARS OPEN FOR MOANS AND GROANS!

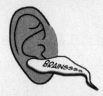

10: KEEP YOUR NOSE ALERT FOR THE STENCH OF RAW SEWAGE MIXED WITH ROTTEN MEAT!

---

[1] In my town, it began at the meatpacking plant. And yes, cows *can* get zombified.

[2] Per the "you are what you eat" rule.

[3] For the record, Mr. Cocoran was kind of a zombie even before he got bitten.

[4] Based on most horror movies. Origin stories for evil monsters always begin with some chemical experiment gone awry.

[5] It seems funny until what you eat tries to eat you.

[6] According to my friend Joe, a total zombie expert.

[7] Think bacon.

[8] The tenth zombie requested "bran." It's likely he just mispronounced "brain," but this could not be verified.

[9] Which makes sense if you think about how much information is stuffed into smart brains.

[10] Based on a blind taste test of brain samples from both couch potatoes and avid readers.

[11] From a study entitled "Zombies Are Just Dumb Meat with Legs."

[12] If you're short, it's best to start with the knees to bring them down to your level.

[13] It should be noted that zombies *were* harmed in the making of this field study. Many zombies.

[14] Don't try this at home, kids.

[15] Zombies aren't too concerned with fashion.

[16] And now you know what to tell your parents when you need more money for the arcade. You're welcome.

THE ADVENTURE OF A LIFETIME BEGINS BETWEEN THE CUSHIONS OF A SOFA....

From debut novelist
HENRY CLARK

When three kids discover a mysterious sofa and a rare zucchini-colored crayon, they embark on a wild quest to save the world from an alien invasion.

Available however books are sold

L B
LITTLE, BROWN AND COMPANY
BOOKS FOR YOUNG READERS
Discover more at lb-kids.com

BOB603

JOIN BEN AND PEARL ON A
WILD ADVENTURE
THAT'S ANYTHING *BUT*
IMAGINARY.

Don't miss Book 4:
THE ORDER OF THE UNICORN
COMING JULY 2014

The Imaginary Veterinary, a chapter book series by
SUZANNE SELFORS

Available however books are sold   LITTLE, BROWN AND COMPANY
BOOKS FOR YOUNG READERS   lb-kids.com   BOB622

MORTAL HEROES.
IMMORTAL ADVENTURES.

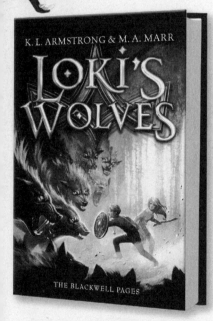

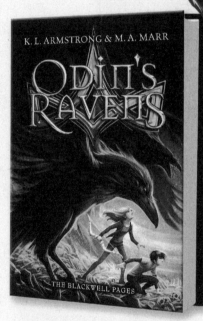

Fantasy, adventure, and Norse mythology collide in this heart-pounding new series from two *New York Times* bestselling authors.

Discover more at **TheBlackwellPages.com**

LITTLE, BROWN AND COMPANY
lb-kids.com

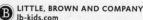
Available however books are sold

BOB636

JT Thomas Photography

PAOLO BACIGALUPI

is the author of *The Doubt Factory*; the highly acclaimed *The Drowned Cities*; and the *New York Times* bestseller *Ship Breaker*, a Michael L. Printz Award winner and a National Book Award finalist. He is also the author of *The Windup Girl* and *Pump Six and Other Stories*, and is the winner of the Hugo, Nebula, Locus, Compton Crook, John W. Campbell Memorial, and Theodore Sturgeon Memorial Awards. He lives in western Colorado with his wife and son.